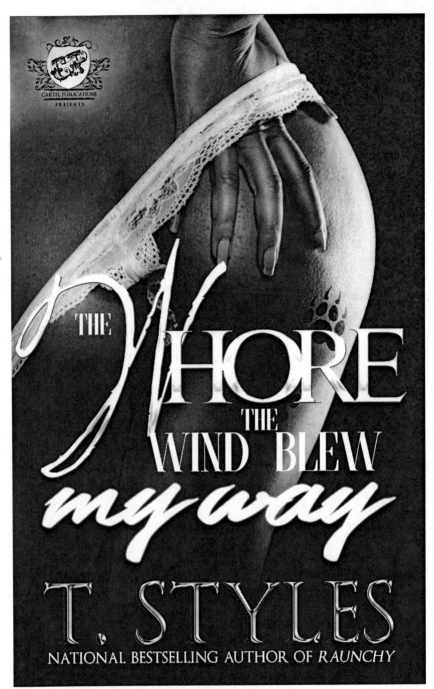

CARTEL PUBLICATIONS
PRESENTS

THE WHORE THE WIND BLEW my way

T. STYLES

NATIONAL BESTSELLING AUTHOR OF *RAUNCHY*

Are You On Our Email List?

Sign up on our website

www.thecartelpublications.com

Or text the word:

Cartelbooks to 22828

For Prizes, Contests, etc.

CHECK OUT OTHER TITLES BY THE CARTEL

PUBLICATIONS

SHYT LIST 1: BE CAREFUL WHO YOU CROSS

SHYT LIST 2: LOOSE CANNON

SHYT LIST 3: AND A CHILD SHALL LEAVE THEM

SHYT LIST 4: CHILDREN OF THE WRONGED

SHYT LIST 5: SMOKIN' CRAZIES THE FINALE'

PITBULLS IN A SKIRT 1

PITBULLS IN A SKIRT 2

PITBULLS IN A SKIRT 3: THE RISE OF LIL C

PITBULLS IN A SKIRT 4: KILLER KLAN

PITBULLS IN A SKIRT 5: THE FALL FROM GRACE

POISON 1

POISON 2

VICTORIA'S SECRET

HELL RAZOR HONEYS 1

HELL RAZOR HONEYS 2

BLACK AND UGLY

BLACK AND UGLY AS EVER

MISS WAYNE & THE QUEENS OF DC

A HUSTLER'S SON

A HUSTLER'S SON 2

THE FACE THAT LAUNCHED A THOUSAND BULLETS

YEAR OF THE CRACKMOM

THE UNUSUAL SUSPECTS

LA FAMILIA DIVIDED

RAUNCHY

RAUNCHY 2: MAD'S LOVE

RAUNCHY 3: JAYDEN'S PASSION

MAD MAXXX: CHILDREN OF THE CATACOMBS (EXTRA RAUNCHY)

KALI: RAUNCHY RELIVED: THE MILLER FAMILY

REVERSED

QUITA'S DAYSCARE CENTER

QUITA'S DAYSCARE CENTER 2

DEAD HEADS

DRUNK & HOT GIRLS

PRETTY KINGS

4   The WHORE The Wind Blew My Way

WWW.THECARTELPUBLICATIONS.COM

By T. Styles   5

The WHORE The Wind Blew My Way

The WHORE The Wind Blew My Way

By

T. Styles

Library of Congress Control Number: 2017936124

ISBN 10: 1945240164

ISBN 13: 978-1945240164

Cover Design: Davida Baldwin www.oddballdsgn.com

www.thecartelpublications.com
First Edition
Printed in the United States of America

What's Up Fam,

I can't believe how fast this year is going by. We're already in March and it seems like time is on speed! We have a lot of new and exciting things planned for this year so make sure you are on our email list and you subscribe to T. Styles' YouTube channel so you won't be left in the dark.

Aight, down to business...*The Whore The Wind Blew My Way* was phenomenal!

T. Styles took it back to the days of, "Raunchy" with this one. In fact, I even told her it put me in the mind of like a "Raunchy", "Shyt List" and "Silence of The Nine" mash up! Trust me when I say you will be pulled in deeply with this novel and be happy to add it to your Twisted T. Styles collection! Get Ready!!

With that being said, keeping in line with tradition, we want to give respect to a vet or trailblazer paving the way. In this novel, we would like to recognize:

Ava DuVernay

Ava DuVernay is the screenwriter and director who brought us, "Selma" and most recently, "Queen Sugar". Which has quickly become one of my favorite new TV shows. Ms. DuVernay has already kicked down a few doors for us African American women by becoming the first to win a Best Director prize at Sundance Film Festival in 2012 for her second feature film, "Middle of Nowhere" as well as being the FIRST African American woman director to be nominated for a Golden Globe for "Selma". Most recently, she became the FIRST African American woman to direct a film with a budget over 100 million dollars. WOW! We at The Cartel Publications and Cartel Urban Cinema are proud to salute Ms. DuVernay and recommend that you check her work out, you won't be disappointed.

Aight, get to it. I'll catch you in the next novel.

Be Easy!

Charisse "C. Wash" Washington
Vice President
The Cartel Publications
www.thecartelpublications.com
www.facebook.com/publishercwash
Instagram: publishercwash
www.twitter.com/cartelbooks
www.facebook.com/cartelpublications
Follow us on Instagram: Cartelpublications
#CartelPublications
#UrbanFiction
#PrayForCeCe
#AvaDuVernay

CARTEL URBAN CINEMA's 2nd MOVIE

MOTHER MONSTER

The movie based off the book,

"RAUNCHY"

by

T. Styles

Now playing on You Tube

Available to Download via VIMEO Soon!

www.cartelurbancinema.com and

www.thecartelpublications.com

CARTEL URBAN CINEMA'S 2nd WEB SERIES

IT'LL COST YOU (Twisted Tales Season One)

NOW AVAILABLE:

YOUTUBE / STREAMING / DVD

www.youtube.com/user/tstyles74

www.cartelurbancinema.com

www.thecartelpublications.com

CARTEL URBAN CINEMA'S 1st WEB SERIES

THE WORST OF US (Season One & Season Two)

NOW AVAILABLE:

YOUTUBE / STREAMING/ DVD

www.youtube.com/user/tstyles74

www.cartelurbancinema.com

www.thecartelpublications.com

CARTEL URBAN CINEMA'S 1st MOVIE

PITBULLS IN A SKIRT – THE MOVIE

www.cartelurbancinema.com and

www.amazon.com

www.thecartelpublications.com

#TheWhoreTheWindBlewMyWay

By T. Styles

15

16   The WHORE The Wind Blew My Way

"Baa-Baa black sheep have you any whores? Yes, sir, yes sir, three rooms full. Some for my master, some for the lames, some for the old men who live down the lane."

The WHORE The Wind Blew My Way

PART ONE

PROLOGUE

PRESENT DAY

The thin mattress squealed under her fragile body and the cheap gold wig she had been forced to wear caused the sides of her cheeks to itch, which summoned a smooth lumpy rash around her angelic face.

Opening her eyes a little, through the rough curls she could see his scowl as he pounded into her flesh, not caring that this moment, like the others, would only add to the nightmares that would torment her life. His position was simple. He had paid for her and he was determined to get his money's worth no matter how violent.

"You like that girl?" He asked, as the weight of his 220-pound body continued to press into her 110-pound frame. Just his heaviness alone caused anguish. "Because I know you like it, now let me hear you tell me." He licked her face, his rough tongue scraping at her jaw.

She smiled a little like she had been taught and nodded rapidly. "Yes...it's...it's nice."

"Good," he smirked, his thrusts slowing in an attempt to make the moment last. "Because you got a future in the business, don't let anybody tell you any different. Unlike some of these bitches you can take dick. That's one thing for sure."

She slammed her eyes closed. "Thank...thank you."

Suddenly she heard a gurgling sound coming from him. Something was definitely wrong. A few moments passed and his body weight pressed into her so hard she could barely breathe. Seconds later the gold wig she wore dampened with a thick, warm wet fluid that oozed into her nose and mouth.

Trembling she kept her eyes shut, wiped her mouth with the back of her hand and hummed a nursery rhyme she'd been taught some time back. *"Baa Baa black sheep have you any whores? Yes, sir, yes sir, three rooms full. Some for my master, some for the lames, some for the old men who live down the lane."*

Suddenly the man's limp, heavy body was pushed off of her and she could breathe again. Cool air rushed up her nostrils soothing her lungs instantly. Rolling to the side she gathered several quick breaths of air.

When she turned back around the person standing before her sent chills down her spine.

CHAPTER ONE
NEW YORK CITY
1974

It was the coldest day of the winter as Louise Smart darted out of the Port Authority, her brown bell-bottoms stained lightly with the cream and blood of the last man she sexed and stabbed earlier that evening.

Ill-prepared for the breath of cold that invaded her tattered tie die blouse, attacking her thin chocolate frame in the process, she pulled her scraggly brown fur coat closed as she stood on the curb and briefly took in the view that was Times Square.

It was spectacular despite the darkness hovering.

Just then a 1973 green Dodge Charger pulled up at the light, it's speakers blasting *Superstious* by *Stevie Wonder*, startling the life out of her. Afraid it was the John she gashed to protect herself an hour earlier, she hid behind a large newspaper stand and waited for the car to drive away. The anticipation was upsetting and it seemed like forever as her heart walloped and sweat poured down her face.

Placing a hand on her chest she whispered, "Please, God, I don't want to die like this…"

When the music faded away and the Charger disappeared up the street she rushed toward the Terminal Bar across the way to meet her next John.

The moment she yanked the door open, she was met with the thick smell of dried piss and smoke as she found two available seats at the crowded bar. Gay black men, loud drunks and every strange character imaginable were present and repping for their city. Using her purse to reserve the seat next to her she ordered two glasses of Monkey Piss from a Jewish bartender with eyebrows as bushy as the copious black hair on his head.

Every time someone entered the bar her gaze would fall to the door, followed by a sigh of relief after realizing it wasn't the man she gouged. It still didn't make her comfortable.

She had to get away.

Now!

"Where are you?" She said to herself. "I can't sit in this bar long." She looked around at the peculiar people in the midst. "It's not safe here."

It seemed like an eternity but five minutes later Hiro Yang, an immigrant from Korea strolled into the bar with extreme confidence. Feeling a little safer when she saw his yellow face, she calmed down, winked and removed her purse so he could take a seat at her side. "What you do this time, Louise?" He asked in a serious tone. "I can't continue to bail you out of trouble. I'm not your fucking man. You know this."

"Aw...come one." She nudged his shoulder playfully. "It's nothing for you to worry about...besides it's Friday night, I'm lonely and I figured you were lonely too. I mean, am I wrong?" She paused. "Can't we make the evening better? Together? Like we always do?"

He looked into her eyes before his gaze fell upon her breasts. "Is that right?" He was suspicious about her motives and rightfully so. "Just a good time, huh? Nothing more?"

"That's all." She winked. "I just missed you, Hiro. That's all it is." She raised her glass and he picked up the other. "To a good time."

"To a good time."

They dinged them together before downing the sweet cocktail inside. "Now...are we gonna do grown folk things in here or leave for a little privacy?" She asked looking at the door again.

"My car's out front, let's go," Hiro reached into his pocket and slammed twenty dollars on the counter.

Way more than what was necessary for the cheap watered down drinks they imbibed. "This place stinks of hopelessness."

"I'm right behind you, daddy," she said as she switched seductively in his direction, capturing the eye of every straight drunk in the building who was sober enough to bare witness to her viscous, luscious curves.

Once outside she eased into his red 1974 Cadillac Coupe Deville with white and cream interior. Now she was in her element and ready to satisfy. Before they even made it to the hotel Louise got to work. Sure he made enough money to rent a room but she fucked him enough to know that part of the appeal for Hiro was being an exhibitionist and the Seduction Doctor always played to her customer's needs.

Excited about what was to come he parked and leaned back into the seat. The new leather groaned under his weight, as he got comfortable. Quickly she undid his blue pinstripe pants, gripped his dick and stroked it until it stiffened in her cream colored palms. Lowering her head she made her mouth extra sloppy and globs of long thick spit ran down the sides of his pole.like white paint.

On some disrespectful shit, he pawed the back of her head and pumped into her throat until his dick was stuffed into her esophagus like a foot in a sock. Hiro could never stand more than two minutes of her head game although he always tried. She was just that good. He knew if she continued at the rate she was going it would be all over in a matter of seconds and he liked it to last.

"Yeah…that's good…suck that shit the way I like it, bitch," he coached, his tongue hanging out the side of his mouth as he looked around to make sure no one was watching. "Yes, just like that you sexy, black bitch. You gotta work for this money today. I ain't gonna just give it to you this time." He paused. "Let me see that pink tongue too." She showed him. "Fuck yes!"

He could say or do what he wanted because she knew she was official with her head game. Besides, the plan was to hit him for the biggest amount of money he'd ever given her so pleasure was a necessity. Within seconds she got it as his thick cream rolled down her throat.

She was done.

Having finished the job, literally, she rose, wiped the corners of her mouth and grinned at him. It was just another day at the office for Louise. He was going for his wallet, preparing to bless her with the usual fifty bucks until, "Hold up, Hiro." She paused. "Now I know you always take care of me but I need a little more tonight."

He fastened his pants but looked at her inquisitively. "How much, Louise? And don't fuck with me. Be straight."

"I'm trying to go to Maryland right away." She reached into her purse and grabbed some tissue and a stick of gum. Wiping her mouth first she tossed the balled up paper in her red pleather bag and then slapped a piece of green gum on her tongue. "I need three hundred dollars and it can't wait."

Hiro smiled and looked out of his window before looking back at her. She blew his high. "You were great, Louise, always have been but you still a whore. A real black one at that, skin the color of a wet New York sidewalk in the rain." He chuckled at his tasteless joke. "And I ain't paid more than forty five dollars for a service from you and I'm not about to start now."

She swallowed the lump in her throat. "I've done something very bad, Hiro and I can't be on the streets. I gotta get away and I gotta do it now. I wouldn't be asking if I had any other choice." She touched his dick. "I know you do good by me so I'm asking for you to do a little more."

He laughed and slapped her fingers away. "You niggers are all the same. Greedy."

"Hiro…"

He reached into his pants, grabbed his wallet and dragged fifty dollars from inside. They were all one-dollar bills from one of the many Laundromats he owned. "That's fifty. Five more than we usually settle on." He tossed the cash into her lap, the dark green color of the bills contrasted against her chocolate thighs.

Tears filled the well of her eyes. "You talk a lot of shit but I know you care about me, Hiro. Why else do you come when I need you? Or pick me up from wherever I am? Don't you see? I'm saying if we can be more it's gotta happen now. Maybe I can stay with you 'til things die down on the streets." Her eyes widened at the possibility. "Maybe in one of your empty houses in Harlem. I've been with you before so I know you got the space. Believe me when I say I don't need much."

He shook his head and wiped his hand down his face. "I can't be with a whore and definitely not a black one, Louise. Besides, what we have may not be conventional but it works for us. Why you wanna go change things all of a sudden?"

"Like I said I need more. And I need it now."

"Well I don't know what to tell you."

"Please, Hiro."

He sighed. "I'm the worst man you could come across, Louise. I know it seems different because of the time we spend but it's true. I'm doing you a favor by not offering you anything more."

She took a deep breath and peeled the money off her thigh. "I have to leave New York. And I'm going tonight. Just know that you'll never see me again." She shook her head. "Guess I did have the wrong impression about you. Have a good evening." She tucked the money into her purse, pushed the door open and diminished into the night.

Tom Gross moved down the narrow hallway bearing Louise's yellow leather suitcase as she ambled behind him. As sweat rolled down his pockmarked skin, he wiped it away, scratching himself in the process. Weighing over three hundred pounds he was far from attractive because he never washed and didn't take care of himself.

Still he deserved an award.

His plans were to do right by Louise and move her to Maryland so that trait deserved her attention and more importantly her time. Besides, he already owned a home in the area and figured a woman was just what he needed to clear up the hoarding lifestyle he grew accustomed to over twenty years.

Excited to take her home, he pushed open the glass door leading out of Louise's building, and wobbled toward his black 1972 Ford pickup truck. A smile was stained on his face as he tossed his new woman's suitcase in the back. After plotting he finally got her and the feeling was astounding.

"I just want you to know this is the right thing," he said pointing a finger at her. "Ain't no life for a pretty thing like yourself on the streets."

She grinned at him appreciatively. "I know, Tom...and thank you for helping a girl out."

When he turned around to help her to the truck he was met across the face with a bat. It bumped his thoughts to another dimension.

WHACK!

Attempting to remove the weapon from Hiro's hand Tom received another blow to the face, which knocked his large body against his truck. Summoning all of the strength he could muster Tom managed to roll off the vehicle and backed into the street to flee the monster. But his weight wouldn't allow swift moves so he dropped to the asphalt, defeated.

Louise was frantic as she surveyed the malicious scene. What was happening? The last time she talked to Hiro he didn't want to be bothered but now he was beating up the one man who was going to help her run away.

With Tom down Hiro rushed up to Louise and grabbed her by the shoulders. "Get in my car. I'll finish him off."

Hands covering her trembling shiny red lips she remained frozen in place. "W...why did you—"

"What do you mean why? I came back for you, to help you!" His eyes were wild and frantic. "Now get in my car and stop asking questions!"

She snatched her suitcase from Tom's truck and turned on the heels of her white go-go boots, to run toward his car and slide into the passenger seat. Hiro plopped into the front seat and was about to drive off until he saw Tom lifting his head from the concrete.

"Why won't you die?" He said to himself. "Fucking die!" He carried on as if the man had done something to him personally.

Louise placed her hand over her heart to calm it down. "Just leave him be, Hiro. Let's go while we can."

"I can't do that...I'm sorry." He had to finish what he started so using his car as a weapon Hiro pulled out of the parking space and ran over Tom's head, forcing an opening at the top of his scalp like a soft melon.

After his car jerked upward, and he looked in the rearview mirror and saw the bloody carcass he was certain Tom wouldn't be getting back up again. And he was right.

"Why all of this?" She asked, holding the sides of her face. "It makes no sense. You...you just ran over a man."

Gazing over at Louise he took a deep breath and placed his vanilla colored cold hand on her warm thigh. "I want you to come with me."

By T. Styles   33

She nodded, still shook by the violent scene. Louise never knew he was that type of crazy, despite the warning he delivered earlier in the day. What had she gotten herself into? "Why...why didn't you just say that? He didn't deserve to be treated like that, Hiro. You went way too far!"

"I don't know why it happened like that." He wiped a hand down his face, wild eyes pushing into the night. "And I don't know why I want you with me." He gripped the steering wheel with his free hand. "I mean, you're a whore Louise and every part of me hates you for it." He removed his hand and placed both of them on the wheel, clutching so tightly his knuckles whitened. "But I hate myself more for...for caring about you."

She took a deep breath.

Since they first laid eyes on each other five years ago she felt in her heart he was the one. Even begged him to get her off the streets every year around Christmas, hoping he would catch the holiday spirit and fulfill the dream she always had, to fall in love. And each time she was met with the same answer.

"Whore's don't get to keep the guy and the money. Fairy tales are for good girls only."

Now she was learning that his response didn't mean he didn't want her in his life. Who could blame him? The inside of her pussy was smooth as expensive silk and her mouth was wet as a whistle. She was worth more to him than he let on and the last thing he wanted was her gone and definitely not forever.

"So what now, Hiro?" She moved uneasily.

Silence.

"Because I can't go back to the streets." She stared at him. "If you're gonna take me you need to keep me."

He nodded. "I know. But life with me is nothing like you can imagine. On the streets we have an understanding, Louise." He gazed at her and then the road. "You take care of me and I take care of you. You don't have to worry about my...my ways and I don't worry about you but..." He paused. "Everything is about to be different if we're going to be together. You will see my darker side."

"I don't care."

"Even if that means not going to Maryland?" He stopped at the light. "Because we gonna be right here. I have too much at stake to leave."

She looked away.

"I don't care about none of that, Hiro. I just need to get off the streets. To keep a low profile."

He was regretting his decision already. In life he moved based on impulse, which almost caused problems for his business. Something told him this was no different. "What did you do? That has you wanting to run? I need the truth."

"I stabbed someone in the thigh who tried to hurt and rape me."

"But you've done that before, Louise. You've shot men and didn't think about leaving town. Just changed your wig and moved on. Why now? Give me honesty."

She glanced at the cars passing in the night and touched her belly. "I'm pregnant. So I can't be this anymore."

Upon hearing her words, his stomach bubbled. For a second he contemplated pumping his brakes and tossing her into the night. "Pregnant? Why didn't you tell me that?" His eyebrows pulled together. "Before I did all this?"

She frowned. "I didn't know you were coming back for me!" She pointed at the back window. "And you just killed the only man who was going to take me away from it all! I had made a decision to move on."

"What did I get myself into?" He shook his head. "Why didn't I just let you go? I could've been home! Dealing with my own problems and my own life." He bared his teeth and slowly looked at her with disdain. "Instead of the whore the wind blew my way."

"Hiro!"

He focused outward and suddenly everything looked drab and colorless. The last thing he wanted to be was a father. "And I'm sure a hoe like you don't even know who the father is." He paused. "No need in pretending you do."

She giggled softly.

"Fuck you laughing for?" He asked.

"Because that's where you wrong, Hiro. You will only need to take one look at my baby's eyes and you'll find that this child belongs to you. That much I'm certain of."

7 MONTHS LATER

Life had been hell for Louise and that moment was no different.

Her life was in danger.

Puddles of sweat rolled down the sides of Louise's face as Hiro hung over top of her, the tip of the knife he already jabbed into her neck tinged with blood. His breaths were heavy and a glob of spit dangled from the corner of his mouth, before dribbling on her naked nine-month pregnant belly.

"Please...don't do this to me." She attempted to remain calm but he was under the influence of LSD. There was no need in making him nervous which exacerbated the matter. "If you kill me you gonna hurt the baby...our baby. I know you don't want that because you'll regret it, Hiro. I promise." She cried. "So...so just put the knife down and lets talk."

"You think for one minute I believe that baby's mine? You think I don't know you trying to put a kid on me so you can get my money? My businesses? My family warned me about you!"

She shook her head rapidly from left to right. "No, Hiro...I promise. That's not what I'm trying to do. I just—"

"SHUT THE FUCK UP! SHUT UP NOW!"

As she sat in fear for her life there was one dread that held above all others. If only her baby had come earlier, she would've taken her chances on the street; maybe find a shelter for families who accept women and children. But as it stood all of the shelters were overflowed and she was in the presence of a mad man hoping to survive. But it wasn't always like that between them.

For months he went back and forth in rage when he got high. Some nights he could be as sweet as everyday sunshine and other moments he was dark as death. And when she threatened to leave, during his sober spots, he would buy the baby another piece of furniture and give Louise a few more dollars to convince her to stay.

In her hope for something better, she fell for it every time despite knowing his kindness never lasted long. *'I want my baby to have a father'*, is what she told friends and now she realized some parents are better off absent from a child's life.

With him, she realized the saying, *'If someone tells you how they are, believe them.'*

"Shut up! Shut up!" He yelled wielding the knife closer to her face, the tip of the blade threatening to end her beauty. "No need in you lying to me. You want my money! Don't you!"

"Hiro, I — "

Suddenly he kicked her in the lower stomach so hard she saw the crown of her baby's head press against the top part of her belly causing her water to break. Her eyes widened and for a second she forgot about the mad man revved up on LSD standing above her. He was no longer a factor and it was time to fight with everything she had.

Rising to her feet she charged him, pushed him backward and rushed past him in an attempt to run for the bathroom. There was no escaping the apartment but she understood that she would be forced to have her only child in the home of a drug addict who didn't want the responsibility of a baby, but was too obsessed to let her go.

As warm water trickled out of her vagina and splashed onto the hardwood floor, she continued to move toward the bathroom. Although he chased her she was almost there. Almost safe. If only she could go faster.

He was a mad man! A lunatic! His ranting and raving didn't stop but inside the bathroom she would have all of the privacy she needed to give birth to her first child. If only she could make it.

Right before she entered, she felt a cool sensation run down the inside of her arm. When she looked down she saw her own blood. Turning around slowly she examined Hiro and realized the knife was weighed heavy in his hand with thick red fluid. He had sliced a chunk of flesh off her left arm and the twinkle in his eyes told her he was happy about it.

But why didn't she feel pain?

There was nothing left to do, she had to kill him or allow him to take her and her baby's life.

Filled with rage Louise charged Hiro, her large belly between them as a life buffer. He may have been cock strong from LSD but she was a woman who was doing all she could to protect her unborn child. In her mind a mother's love trumped any narcotic and she was set on proving her theory correct.

Using her fists and arms, she pushed him hard and he fell into the table. Wanting to gain control she crawled on top of him, and hammered his head repeatedly into the hardwood floor. She was a woman and he was a man but her violent behavior confused him and for the moment made her stronger.

"GET OFF ME!" He yelled. "YOU CRAZY!"

When he moved a little, almost knocking her off his body, she slapped his hand and then the knife got free, spinning on the floor like a coin. Quickly she seized the knife and before he knew it she crawled back on top of him and sliced him in the arm, legs and face.

"YOU WON'T HURT MY BABY! YOU WON'T HURT MY BABY!" She yelled, each word ending in a rip at his skin.

She made an error in judgment. With each thrust tears rolled down her face as she realized he was no different from the other Johns she dated, secretly nurturing a fetish that had nothing to do with love, but more their hate and lust for prostitutes. She didn't stop flailing her arms until he was passed out; barely breathing and her contractions grew heavier.

It was time to give birth.

Slowly she rose to her feet and moved toward the bathroom. Using the wall to remain standing, she left bloody handprints over them. Pushing the door open she locked it, eased down on her knees and crawled to the tub. Holding her belly with one hand she turned the water on and willed herself inside. Partially nude anyway, she removed her wet underwear and tossed them out of the tub. They slapped against the tile a few feet out. She didn't feel much pain in her arm because adrenaline coursed through her veins.

It was time to give life.

1 YEAR LATER

"Girl, you don't think I know this cat a psycho?" Louise asked her friend Mellie as they sat on the sofa, watching Sanford & Son on a wooden floor model TV. An ashtray filled with two lit cigarettes gave off so much smoke in the living room it was difficult for them to see one another clearly. "But what can I do? I need the money and that little girl in that room needs food." She pointed at the door where her baby slept. "Nothing gonna prevent me from caring for her that's for sure."

Mellie lifted her cigarette, smudged with red lipstick and placed it between her yellowing teeth to hold it in steady. "All I'm saying is if it was me he'd be getting pussy from somewhere else." She inhaled the smoke and tapped the long ash into the glass ash trey before exhaling. "Even ho's got standards, Louise."

Louise heard her friend but shit was difficult for her these days. With Hiro being arrested for attempted murder, she was the sole provider for their baby Kaysa.

The woman was also focused.

Her plan was to save up two hundred more dollars and move both of them to Maryland where she heard the possibilities were better. To Maryland, where she always wanted to live. But first she had to suck and fuck a few more dicks to secure her travel plans and she was going to do just that.

Sure her next client was dangerous and she understood why Mellie didn't like Chuck, the trick she had lined up for the night. Rumor had it that he had been known to do a little more than fuck the whores he encountered in his travels. Just last week while sleeping with white girl Cheryl, he removed his dick and stabbed her in the pussy with a knife when she wasn't looking just to hear her scream. She landed in the hospital and died three days later.

Authorities couldn't prove he was responsible because nobody in the prostitute community would say a word but they all had their opinions.

He was a nut.

So why fuck him? Louise's dilemma was simple. He paid deep for the women he liked and sometimes the money was enough to pay rent at her cheap apartment. Being a whore meant putting your life on the line so to her some tricks were worth the risks.

"Let me worry about myself, Mellie." She sighed. "If he tries to hurt me I'll gut him like the rest. Nobody's separating me from my baby girl. She's gonna grow up to know that I was there." She grinned and looked upward. "That's for sure."

Mellie laughed as Louise ambled to the window, pushed back the thick cream curtain and gazed outside. As she looked into the dark night for her John she sighed heavily. Where was he? She had two hours to fuck him and get back in time to take Kaysa to Miss Wayland's, her real babysitter in the building.

Miss Wayland was an out of work schoolteacher who murdered a janitor after catching him stashing a little girl in the supply closet at the school to rape her on his breaks. The trial went on for months, with the money for her defense being funded by people who felt she stood for what was right by saving the little girl. But that was five years ago and when the publicity died down so did her funds, forcing her to rely on whores and single mothers who cared enough to scrape up a few bucks to have their children in her protective care. At two years old the babies in her home could read.

Yes, Louise certainly wanted more for Kaysa, which was a world away from her own mother who was un-affectionately known as Nasty Pussy Gladys.

When Louise was ten-years old she watched her mother make art out of dick sucking. Sitting at a kitchen table, Louise was in awe of her reckless mama. And having to slam her hand down on the thick brown roaches, which were trying to crawl into her cereal, didn't distract her in the least.

In her young mind her mother was a star.

She was amazed at the comfort Gladys exhibited when she serviced men out in the open. Men would walk in angry but within minutes under Gladys' touch they'd soften like melting ice, with whimpering voices resembling women. In Louise's eyes she was a magic woman and she wanted to be just like her.

She could always tell when her mother was doing a great job, when the men's eyes would roll to the back of their heads and they'd moan so loudly Gladys would have to slap a hand over their quivering lips to prevent them from letting the neighborhood know about her good-good.

The milkman, whose body was pressed against the refrigerator, at the moment, was no different. On her knees, she gave him two minutes of her signature deep throat session in which she proved that no matter the dick size it could still disappear down her throat.

She was a magician of sorts.

And it showed.

But this was a family affair. For Louise, although young, had a responsibility too. It was her duty to make sure her drunken father Bruce didn't wake up before the cognac he sucked down earlier in the day wore off. If he did awaken from his slumber Louise's job was to rush and let her mother know.

He may have known what his wife was doing to pay the bills, evident by the conversations Louise overheard, but seeing this wife in action was another monster. He bought into her lies that she was doing it just for the money and after they saved up enough she would stop.

All lies.

Time may have passed and the sun may have set but Gladys didn't feel a need to give up her whorish ways. But it didn't mean Louise couldn't be saved with a little intrusion. The evolution happened when one day Donna, Gladys' sister, came over the house uninvited only to catch Louise alone, giving fake oral sex to one of her dolls.

Without any questions Donna snatched her niece from the home believing she was only reenacting the whorish performance she'd learned from her sister. Donna determined in that moment that Louise's life would be different so she separated mother and child forever. Had it not been for the weekly phone calls, Gladys would not know her child was alive.

But there was a problem. Whoring was in Louise's veins and within time she found her way to the carnal light. It happened when Anderson, Donna's live in boyfriend, one morning across the breakfast table, noticed Louise's budding breasts. Louise immediately caught his lustful looks and used the art of seduction she learned from her mother to drive him crazy in small flirtatious bouts.

At that moment to let him know she was interested she leaned over her plate, causing her breasts to mash into the pancakes, smearing syrup all over her chest.

Her games didn't stop there.

Whether it would be walking around the house in tight blue jean shorts with her ass cheeks hanging out or "forgetting" the door was open as she showered so he could see her naked body, she did it all but still it was not enough.

She desired excitement. More of an adventure.

So when Donna ran to the grocery store she made a proposition to her aunt's man. For fifteen dollars she would allow him to kiss her breasts. When that wasn't good enough she raised the game to thirty dollars and sat on his face as he jerked off.

Mentally damaged at a young age, it brought her a sick sense of pride knowing she was as powerful as her mother and men would weaken at her fingertips. Gladys once told her that there was nothing sexier in the world than hearing a man moan and she agreed.

Before long Donna's man wanted more and would rough her up a little when she refused to play their games. Louise may have been too scared to have sex but everything else was on the table when he was nice to her and gave her money. For months they carried on in secret until Donna came home early, after getting a call from the high school that Louise had missed another day.

With her hands filled with groceries, she got nauseous when she opened her bedroom door, only to see Louise sitting on her fiancé's lap; his hands on her waist while his tongue slithered down her throat like a garden snake.

"What the fuck are you doing?" She yelled dropping the bags to the floor. "To my niece?"

"She…she was seducing me, Donna!" He said, wide eyes with guilt. "I told you not to let her live here and now look! She's a slut and I'm so weak! Please forgive me!"

The family bond she shared with her niece was severed in that moment.

Donna yanked Louise off his lap by her hair and tossed her into the entertainment system like she weighed nothing. It toppled on top of her small body, causing gashes from the shattered glass to dig into the flesh of Louise's back and legs. But if it were sympathy that the youngster wanted she would have to look elsewhere.

Donna beat Louise so badly she broke her jaw, both of her arms and her right leg; all while Anderson stood back and watched. His reason for not interfering was clear. As long as *she wasn't taking her anger out on him he was okay. To hell with the teenager who he used since he realized she was searching for something. She was searching for love.*

With the damage done, and while she was barely conscious, Donna tossed Louise out on the street, forcing her into homelessness. Ironically the beating was the best and worst thing that could've happened in that moment. Because despite the painful hospital stay it was the only reason she wasn't on the street. Being bed ridden meant a warm place to stay and three meals but even that wouldn't last.

She needed to make amends.

For days Louise called Donna trying to apologize but her calls went unanswered. The woman was a savage. She wanted nothing to do with her niece for seducing her man. She was cut off. When trying to reach her aunt personally didn't work she resorted to calling her downstairs neighbor, eventually convincing her to talk to Donna to at least get her mother's number. She figured if she didn't want her at the house that maybe Gladys would take her back. But all attempts failed because Donna didn't want her in her life. Not only that, she was too embarrassed to admit that she had failed raising her niece, to the point of making things worse.

Louise was on her last day in the hospital when she overheard the doctor telling a nurse that since no one claimed the teenager, she would be admitted into a group for adolescents that evening. Having heard bad stories about those places, which included gang rapes and murders, she got dressed and hitchhiked a ride to her aunt's house. Broken and displaced she figured if Donna saw her banged out face she'd take pity on her and at least give her a few bucks. But when she reached the house she discovered Donna moved with no forwarding address.

Her world collapsed.

Broke.

Alone.

And scared...

She turned her first full trick with an old white man who hated himself for loving black women; especially those with skin the color of melted chocolate. It didn't stop him from picking her up and once he had her in his car humiliating her incessantly.

"Look at you...you ain't nothing but a dirty nigger." He glared over at her, and then focused on the road again. "Aren't you?"

"Yes, sir," she would say quietly, body trembling.

"You like white men, nigger girl?" When her response was inaudible he yelled, "Open your mouth!"

"Yes, sir," She responded remembering how her mother said less and did more when she serviced men. "I do like white men. Very much."

"I know you do."

This went on for minutes and when she gazed at his crotch, she saw he was hardening in his blue slacks with every brutal word. She was relieved when he finally released his penis and stroked it to a full stiffness because at least she didn't have to hear his voice any longer. His words were painful and attacked a part in her soul she was too young to comprehend.

He parked. "Get over here," he demanded. "Hurry up." He looked out to see who was watching. No one was around. "If you move any slower I'm gonna hurt you."

Swiftly she complied.

Although she was still a virgin she figured he wouldn't hurt her too badly. Besides, her mother had sex with strange men all the time and it didn't injure her body. She figured it would be gross at the most but that was it. Until he slammed her on top of him, opening her vagina in ways that were unnatural and forceful. He tore at her flesh for his pleasure even though she begged him to stop.

He didn't.

The suffering lasted all of ten minutes but in the moment it felt like a lifetime.

Satisfied he tossed the small change her way and said, "Get out. If you lucky I put a baby in you. It'll be worth something too."

She looked down at the money. Her virginity was worth $33.00 and tears streamed down her cheek. Still, she left the car, gladly.

As she walked down the street she thought about her mother. How could she like something so painful? She was confused as her view of the world shattered in a sweaty, funky moment.

Sore, humiliated and unable to use her body for profit for days, she bummed more money by relying on the fact that she was still a teenager in need of food and shelter. Placing her long black hair in two Afro puffs, she found an empty Pork & Beans can and asked for money everywhere she went. Mostly men would help because women, especially if they were with their spouses, considered her budding breasts and curves a threat.

And they were right.

After awhile, the cash allowed her to rent a seedy motel room for a couple of nights or so that was the plan.

Even whores needed structure so she stayed another week, turning tricks more regularly when her body healed up. She taught herself how to deal with different personalities and was quickly a favorite for men who wanted a woman with a tender body and pretty face. The weeks became months and before long she gave that shithole of a room the next ten years of her life.

When Chuck's car pulled up Louise turned around to address her friend. That quickly Mellie removed heroin from her purse and was cooking it up on the living room table. "You want some, girl? I can get you right before you leave. I gotta little extra."

Louise stomped toward her and looked down at the dope. "You know I don't fuck around and I told you not to do it around me." She glared and pointed at her. "Are you gonna be able to watch my kid?"

Mellie shrugged. "Look you asked me to babysit remember?" She grimaced. "I told you I was off early tonight and wanted to relax. I'm doing you a favor."

"I know you told me but...not while you on the shit, Mellie." She paused. "Kaysa sleeps through the night but—"

"Look, I'm grown, Louise! If you don't want none that's fine by me. To each his own. To be honest I don't see how you fuck with a clear mind anyway." She tied the brown rubber tourniquet around her arm and tapped her vein. "After the things I've seen I need a bump. You should too..."

Louise considered what she said and sighed.

At one point she loved being in the streets but that all changed when she found out she was having a baby. Now it was all about Kaysa and her safety and in her opinion she was compromising her security by leaving her friend in her home.

"You want me to leave or what?"

"Fuck all that, Mellie. You better not be doing that shit in front of my baby."

Mellie pushed the long needle into the heroin drenched cotton and then her vein. With a slack jaw, dripping with spit she said, "She'll be fine, girl. What you need to be concerned with is yourself." Her head dropped backward. "And your...your..."

Her speech drifted off.

If Louise didn't need the money she would've put Mellie out and told Chuck to kick rocks too. But that scenario wasn't an option. Besides, Kaysa was asleep and she figured even a dope fiend could watch a sleeping baby for a couple of hours. Right? So she took a deep breath, said a silent prayer and pressed into the night.

Two hours later Louise stumbled through the building's door as if the Brooklyn Bridge was on her shoulders. Her John was not aggressive but it took him forever to get hard and cum. The only bright side was that he gave her a little extra money for her trouble and now exhausted, her head could do nothing but hang low as she trudged upwards, the yellow scarf she carried dusted against the grungy steps. She had no energy but figured seeing her daughter would at least force a smile on her face. It had in the past.

And then she heard voices.

Stern voices with deep baritones that belonged to men of authority. From her position she could now see her apartment door was ajar and the bottoms of dark blue pants hanging over large shiny black patent leather shoes walked across her living room floor. Confused, she dashed up the stairs and into her apartment.

It was a madhouse surrounding a massacre.

Police officers were everywhere and no one seemed to respect the owner who was now present. "What's going on?" She yelled walking up to one officer. "Why are you in my house?"

Vociferous sounds continued and she could smell gunpowder mixed with the metallic odor of blood in the air. Something went terribly wrong.

"Are you Louise Smart?" A white officer who was accompanied by a larger policeman asked.

Louise looked at them confused, unable to move and unable to make sense of what was happening. Her eyes bulged as she attempted to gaze over their shoulders, at the investigators working feverishly on someone covered in blood on the floor. A person she was certain was her friend Mellie.

For a second she recalled the police cars out front but it was no big deal in her neighborhood. On any given day she would see officers storming in and out her building looking for perps or participating in some sort of raid.

That night was different.

"Where's my daughter?" She said in an agitated whisper. "Where...where is she?"

"Did you know the person over there?" The officer asked in an attempt to control the situation.

Louise could barely see the body but she knew whom they were referring too. "If...if it's Mellie yes, I did. But what happened?"

"Someone murdered her," the officer said, as if he were talking about takeout food. "That's what happened."

Louise could no longer use her legs and dropped to the floor. "What? But why?"

"We aren't sure but neighbors recall her yelling the name Marvin Jr." He paused. "We were hoping you could shed some light on the matter. All we can tell you now is that someone kicked in the door and shot her multiple times in the face."

Her guts felt like they were boiling as they bubbled in her belly. She knew exactly who Marvin Jr. was. He was the son of the man she stabbed over a year ago and somehow he found her. The guilt she felt in that moment weighed her down. This could not be happening.

"I don't know...who could've...who could've..." Suddenly allowing her to watch her precious daughter seemed dumb. Although if she had been home Marvin Jr. would have killed her instead, which was his plan. "I'm sorry...but I...I don't feel too well."

"Ma'am...do you know anything about what happened here tonight or not?" The officer said more forcefully.

"No...I...don't." She took a deep breath and tried to pull herself together. Mellie wasn't the first whore friend she lost to the streets and she certainly wouldn't be the last. She had to remain calm because she would need all of her energy for her child. "My daughter...where is she?" When they didn't respond she stood up and looked around. "I said where is my child?"

"In our custody."

Her eyes widened and she placed her hand over her throat. "But why…is she hurt?"

"No, but we saw the drugs, ma'am. We aren't sure why the deceased was killed but we have to hold your child for evaluation, to make sure she wasn't harmed in any way. They'll determine at that time if they will return her to your custody."

"No, you don't understand…without my child…without her I die." Her body rocketed. "Please, sir give her back to me. I'll be moving I promise."

"Should've thought about that before you left her with that…person."

Louise looked around. "So, are you saying there's a possibility that…that I won't get her back? That…that she'll be taken from me forever?"

"That's exactly what we're saying."

Louise broke down and cried from her soul.

6 MONTHS LATER

Louise left Christian's diner after failing yet again to secure gainful employment, the one thing necessary to get her child back. She hadn't even turned a trick in months electing to use the money she saved to get a new apartment in a nicer, but still ghetto, neighborhood.

Still, things were not working out for her.

Broke, lonely and out of ideas, she was doing her best to keep her sanity. From the moment she decided to have her child, as opposed to making an appointment with Amanda who scraped at women's insides in her basement to abort pregnancies, she was focused on doing right by Kaysa. She didn't want her walking the earth without her, knowing that in order to grow into a responsible young lady, she needed a good example.

She needed a *good* mother.

The moment she stepped on the curb a black car pulled up in front of her, it's driver a stout black man with sex on his mind. His eyes roamed over her body and to Louise it felt like he fucked her already. "Hey, foxy mama. Want a ride 'cause if you do I sure don't mind?"

"No, I'm fine." She tried to walk around the car but he pulled up a few inches, blocking her path and almost running over her feet.

"You sure?" He removed a stack of money from his pocket. "I'm a paying man and I heard the weather will be bad soon." He looked upward at the cloudy sky. "Would hate for you to get wet if you don't wanna." He licked his lips.

She frowned. "I'm positive. Now fuck off." She stomped around his vehicle and towards Hiro's car, which she kept after he was locked up. It was the only thing she owned that was in her name and she was certain that soon she would have to sell that for funds.

Louise was driving down the street when suddenly she cried heavily, large tears falling onto her navy blue dress. Life was bearing down on her and it didn't seem as if time was on her side. First the son of someone she wronged over a year ago murdered her friend and now the government had taken her daughter away.

Pulling up in font of the apartment building, she wiped her tears and took a deep breath before getting out. It was important to pull her self together. The last thing she needed was her nosey neighbor's creating lies about the reason for her pain. As she took a moment to regain her composure something became obvious. It's not as if she'd forgotten what suddenly popped into her mind but she had tried to convince herself that she could change. That she could be a different person.

At the end of the day she was a whore and a whore needed to satisfy not only to make a living but also to feel important, and to survive.

When she finally entered her home and opened the fridge, she was angry that it was bare. She hadn't bothered to eat in days and now that her stomach was tugging and pulling and she was broke, she realized she'd have to wait even longer before a meal came her way.

"God, help me...please. All I want is my daughter back. Show me the way or stand back while I go back to what comes natural to me."

KNOCK. KNOCK. KNOCK.

Louise opened the door only to see her landlord standing on the other side. He was a thick white man who had more hair on his neck than his head. He was definitely a character but most of all he got on her nerves since she'd arrived at the apartment complex and she could tell by the snide look on his face that the moment would not be different. "How you doing, Louise?" He licked his lips.

"What do you want?"

"You got three days. Otherwise it's the pussy or the rent." He chuckled and his eyes slowly rolled over her voluptuous body. "And you already know what I want because I've made myself clear."

She sighed. "I'll pay the rent, Mark..." She attempted to close the door when he blocked it with a stiff arm.

"Hold up, Louise because the last thing you want is to treat a man badly who can help you." He took one step inside.

"Excuse me?"

"You look like you're having a bad day and I have an idea on how I can make things better." He rubbed his chin and his eyes rested on her breasts. "You wanna get high?"

She frowned and rolled her eyes. "I'm not a burn out, Mark...and you know I don't fuck around with drugs."

He laughed. "Look, I know a ho when I see one so pardon me for coming at you in an honest way. Let me approach this differently." He pointed at her. "You get high with me now, fuck me whenever I want and I'll make you my wife. I'll be good to you, never disrespect you and make you a happy woman. And judging by how empty this apartment is because you probably sold everything for profit, I think that's a good deal. Don't you?"

She laughed hysterically. It was the first chuckle she had in months and she was suddenly grateful for the idiot's presence. "Now why on earth would I want you anywhere near my body, let alone my life?"

"Maybe because I own this building?"

She shrugged. "So what?" She crossed her arms over her chest.

"And you don't have your kid."

She uncrossed her arms. "Who told you that?"

"Do yourself a favor. Don't go to the bar with the chicks in this building when something's on your mind, even if they paying." He pointed at her again. "They talk too much. Take that from me, I know."

She rolled her eyes and stomped to the sofa before flopping down. It was in such bad shape her butt sank to the floor. He pushed the closing door open and followed, his eyes on her thick ass the entire time.

"I don't know what to do, Mark." She threw her face in her hands. "I can't get a job to take care of my daughter and I'm afraid I'll lose her to the system. At this point I don't know what to do."

He sat next to her and placed his clammy hand on her thigh before removing a heroin bag from his jean pocket. Waving it he said, "What would you do if I told you I could make all your troubles go away? Would you take the time to believe me?"

She shook her head from left to right because she felt herself growing weak. In the past she said no and meant it but life had gotten her down. Could she be one in a million whom could actually break the habit after trying it once? "I can't do this. Please don't make me."

"Come on, Louise." He looked around. "What else you got? The bottom is already there, all you have to do is step down."

6 MONTHS LATER

Louise was standing in the middle of her fake husband's living room floor, body frail and eyes hollow. The social worker, a thin black woman with crusted grey lips held the stroller handle holding Kaysa with authority. She knew she was in full control of the situation and she had every intention on letting it be known.

Louise, on the other hand, couldn't help but eye her beautiful little girl who sat peacefully inside. Her Asian eyes were bright and she had so much thick black curly hair on her scalp it looked fake, almost doll like. What grabbed Louise's attention the most was that as she stared at her only child, baby Kaysa appeared to love being observed. She cooed, grabbed her feet and smiled every time someone gazed her way, as if she were performing.

The Social worker cleared her throat. "I'm gonna be straight. Why do you want your child back?"

Louise's mouth hung open because she hadn't expected her question. She rubbed at her throat and said, "Uh…because she's mine."

"That's not a good enough answer."

With wide eyes she looked everywhere but at the woman's face. "I want her back because I miss her.

Because I haven't been the same since she was taken from me."

"What about a job? Do you have one?"

"Uh...yes," Mark interjected, running to the living room table where he doctored fake paystubs. He picked them up and handed them to the social worker who took forever examining the documents.

She looked up and sighed, "Well things look okay here." She stuffed them in her briefcase.

Mark walked closer to Louise and rested his arm on her shoulder, to oversell their fake relationship. "Thank you," he said. "Me and my wife just want the best for our daughter."

The social worker nodded. It was apparent she enjoyed the perceived power she had over the situation so she took her time with what Louise wanted to know.

Would she or would she not return mother to child?

"That's good because even though Louise has a job working in this building with you, it doesn't make her a good mother."

"Excuse me?" Louise snapped.

"Hear me out," the social worker continued. "Kaysa will need care. Lots of it. She can hardly sleep at night and she'll need a strong emotional support system over the next couple of days. Only God knows what she witnessed the night your friend was murdered, Louise."

Mark laughed. "She was a baby, she doesn't remember anything." He paused. "Trust me...she'll be better now that she has her mother again. That I'm certain of, especially if I have anything to do with it."

"Well you don't have anything to do with it." The social worker frowned. "And if you don't think a child knows a terrible situation when she sees one you're foolish and shouldn't be caring for—"

"No!" Louise interjected, stepping away from Mark's heavy arm. "You're right children do know. And I want you to know Kaysa will be loved and in a peaceful home." She placed a hand over her thumping heart. "Give her back to me and I promise nothing will happen to her. With me as her mother she will grow into a well-rounded young lady. She will know the sky is the limit and I will make sure that she has a strong role model at her side. Please, return my baby to me. I'm begging you."

The social worker looked at her for what seemed like an eternity. "I hear you about being a well rounded woman but right now, in this moment, she's a little girl," she said really driving her point home. "Which means she's impressionable. There are to be no drugs or violence around her whatsoever." She pointed at both of them. "So I must ask...are either of you using now?"

"What?" he coughed. "Of course not."

The social worker looked at both of them longer. "And you, Louise?"

"Never," Louise responded. Louise tried to conceal her anger because the baby belonged to her but it was hard. The woman was stretching the agonizing moment forever.

"Are you ready to be a mother, Louise?"

Louise stepped closer to her. "Like I said, I won't let anything happen to *my* child, I promise."

The social worker clapped her hands together. "Well, I've seen enough for now. Congratulations and I'll be in contact." She touched the top of Kaysa's head, as if she wanted to say...*POOR, POOR BABY.* Afterwards she clapped once more, smiled and walked out.

When the social worker left Mark locked the door as if the woman was a thug nigga about to reenter and relieve him of his money.

Louise, on the other hand, gazed at Kaysa who was playing happily with a pink stuffed elephant. "You're perfect," she said as a tear rolled down her cheek. "And I'm going to do right by you. I just...I just..."

Mark grabbed Louise's hand, "You ready to get right?"

"I don't know, Mark. Maybe I shouldn't. Since she's here."

"You can go clean afterwards. For now feed your habit one last time."

"I can't."

He frowned. "You know what, stupid bitch...be dumb then! But I'm going to take care of myself." He walked toward the room and slammed the door.

As she watched him leave she thought about her predicament. Who was she fooling? For several months she had been addicted to heroin so there was no way she could stop cold turkey.

True, drugs couldn't be a part of her life if she wanted to keep her daughter but right now...well...right now she would indulge. Just a little.

Things had definitely changed in her life.

Kaysa may have been her first love before she was taken but now her life was divided and suddenly the little girl wasn't the sole owner of her mother's heart. Heroin had dug its pointed claws into Louise's world and both mother and daughter would feel its impact.

So she followed her *Convenience Husband* into the backroom, slamming the door behind her self.

And Kaysa?

Well she stayed in that stroller, in her soiled pamper, for two days straight.

High and pushing two-year old Kaysa in a stroller, Louise begrudgingly found herself in the grocery store shopping for her fake husband who didn't understand that their marriage was a ruse. She was a miserable woman and she realized she made many mistakes.

Living with Mark was a complete hell and the worse of them.

He blackmailed her into sex, into cooking and just recently he charged her with getting money since they shot up most of the rent from the tenants. In the beginning she didn't complain but after awhile he grew unreasonable in his requests.

Overnight he became her pimp and a bad one at that.

What was worse was that one refusal from Louise and he threatened to tell New York Child Protective Services that she was an addict. Several times she called his bluff and begged him to call. Besides, sometimes she told herself Kaysa would be better off without her but whenever she tried to give her up her selfishness would not allow her to be raised by another woman. Not when beneath the addiction, sat a person capable of being the best.

And still, her hopes for being a good mother sunk even lower when recently she found out that Mark lost his building due to foreclosure and they had to move in a month.

Hindsight was definitely twenty-twenty. Louise learned quickly that accepting Mark's help was not worth the struggle especially considering she had to prostitute for the three of them now.

To make the self imposed burden heavier, heroin had taken so much of her time that she only had fleeting moments for being a mother, which were few and far between. Just last night she wished she could go back to the time Hiro offered to take her to get an abortion because she would certainly say yes.

"I don't want to be a mother," she'd constantly tell herself. And then she'd look into Kaysa's big beautiful eyes and take it all back. "There has to be a reason for you. For your life." She looked up to the sky. "God...if you love me give me a way to get clean and make your purpose definite. Because right now I'm so confused."

As Louise looked around the aisle in the grocery store for Mark's requested Hamburger Helper, she was relieved when she finally found it. Grabbing two boxes she stuffed them under her musty smelling arm and slogged toward the register, pushing the stroller along the way.

She was annoyed when a black woman with a huge grey bush stepped in front of the stroller, gazed down at it and smiled. "Aw, is your little bugger hiding?"

High from shooting up earlier and with eyes half closed Louise said, "What, lady?" She scratched her ashy nose. "I'm busy right now."

The woman cleared her throat. "I was asking about your baby...where is it?" She frowned.

Thinking the woman had gone mad Louise looked into the stroller herself, only to discover the woman was correct. Kaysa, her only child, was gone.

Louise felt dizzy. "Wait...wait...my baby!" She looked around where she stood like a maniac. "Where is my baby?" She screamed before dropping the boxes of Hamburger Helper on the floor. "Somebody got my baby! Help! Please help, she's gone!"

"Where was she last?" The old lady asked. "Does your husband have her maybe?"

"MOVE, BITCH!" She yelled. "I GOTTA FIND MY KID!"

Besides, the worse possible scenario happened. After asking God to give her a definitive answer on how to handle her child, he took her away. The realization sobered her up quickly. She wanted to be a mother and now she was gone. "Where is my baby? Somebody in this store has my baby!"

Upon hearing that a child had been stolen in their midst, the employees and customers stopped what they were doing to help find Kaysa. But in the end they would realize what the kidnapper already knew.

Little baby Kaysa was gone.

Forever.

A LITTLE LATER

Terrance 'The Wino' ripped through the streets, a two-year-old girl with Asian-eyes stuffed inside his pea green trench coat like a stolen radio. He didn't slow down until he happened upon a block of row homes in Harlem, miles away from the grocery store where he snatched Kaysa. He couldn't believe his luck. Stealing the beautiful little girl was the easiest job he ever pulled off. Besides, Louise nodded out so much in the aisle that he figured she didn't want the kid anyway. So if he could make a little money off her, in his drunken mind, he would be well within his thief rights.

Now it was time for business.

His thoughtless proposal to unsuspecting customers was weird but years of alcohol, with zero sober periods, fucked with his mind. She was no different from a new watch. She was product and he needed the perfect pervert to buy a little girl with no questions asked and he hoped he'd find one when he walked upon a group of men harmonizing in the darkness.

"Say, man, anybody wanna buy a kid?" The Wino spit in his hand and smoothed Kaysa's thick black hair backwards. A few of her short curls popped lazily out anyway. Her light skin was flushed and still her beauty shined despite the filthy wino auctioning away her soul.

What was he doing with her? They thought.

Clueless, as always Kaysa smiled brightly when all eyes were on her. Immediately the men took to the child, which brought attention to the situation. They stopped singing and looked at him, some with their heads tilted and jaws hung.

But it was the lead singer who stepped away from the crowd. "Where you get that kid?"

The Wino sneered. "Don't worry about that, you want it or not, man?"

The lead singer looked at his friends. "It? So it's an object now?"

"You know what I mean."

"Look, get out of here, jive turkey before we stomp you out. We don't want no trouble from the fuzz on account of you. 'Cause I know you not supposed to have her. She too clean."

"Fuck off then!" The Wino yelled.

Angry and still broke, he took the child to a few more spots and the answer was the same, no one wanted to be bothered with the drunk or the stolen child. He was about to give up and knock her over the head with a brick before dumping her in a garbage bin when out of the darkness a pimp they called Ajax from Baltimore appeared.

The light from the lamppost shined against his huge muscular physique and revealed his evil eyes. He had taken many lives that the Wino was certain of. The white button down long sleeve shirt he wore opened just enough to expose his chest hair and his burgundy bell-bottoms were so tight they looked as if they were about to pop. His hair was fine as cat hair and slick backward.

Brushing his hair backward Ajax blocked the wino's path. "What you doing with that kid?" He looked at the child's Asian eyes and then hair. "She don't look like she belong to you." He stopped grooming.

"You can buy her if you want." He held the child in the air like young Simba from the movie Lion King.

"Well where you get her from?"

"Uh...she's my sister's child." He kissed Kaysa with his dry lips on the forehead, forcing her into a forceful cry. Luckily for all she settled down quickly. "She cute ain't she?" He grinned, his lips in a tight straight line. "She gonna be good to somebody that's for sure."

Ajax looked at him suspiciously. "Well what you want for her?"

The wino smiled. "Two hundred dollars."

Ajax grinned. "I'll give you twenty and let you leave with your teeth. Deal or not?"

The Wino took a deep breath and observed his potential customer. The offer for Kaysa was way less than he hoped for but his senses told him the man was evil and he was right. In town on murder business, Ajax was headed back to Baltimore when he saw the exotic looking child. Taking one more life wouldn't hurt him in the least because he wanted the girl.

"Uh...I can get more money if I—"

"Die?" Ajax questioned. "Because if you don't hand over the kid you gonna die, right here, right now."

The Wino nodded so hard his head was about to pop off. "Uh...the money works for me." Ajax gave him the cash and the wino handed him the child. "She clean too. Ain't touched her little pussy one bit except to peak at it."

Ajax's jaw twitched, his brows lowered and the Wino took off running in fear for his life. With the little girl in his possession Ajax bopped away and propped her in the passenger seat of his black Camaro. He pushed the button to open his glove compartment and placed money inside before closing it. Next he placed his brown bristle brush in his lap. Lastly, while looking at the child's face, he released his penis and jerked off. With his cum in hand he smoothed it on her hair like gel, brushed it backward and smiled.

"You're perfect."

Clueless, the baby continued to grin.

Satisfied, he fixed his pants and headed on the road toward Baltimore with one hand on Kaysa to prevent her from flying forward and the other on the steering wheel. It took three hours to make it home with the kid safely.

Once parked, Ajax scooped her up and walked her into a dilapidated building in East Baltimore. Heading downstairs he removed his key and entered the door of an apartment, which was previously a laundry room. This was a piss hole of a spot if ever there was one. There was no bedroom and an area off to the right had a toilet and kitchen in an unfinished hole in the wall. It wasn't big enough for one man let alone two and a child.

When the door closed Lennon yelled from the kitchen. "Where were you, Ajax? Dinner's almost ready! I'm just about to take the meatloaf out the oven. I thought I would have to—"

"Mellow out and come over here for a sec. I want to show you something." Ajax looked down at the little girl and waited for Lennon to appear.

Five seconds later Lennon slid over to him and paused like a mannequin as he saw the little girl in his arms. If Ajax was a scary man to look at Lennon was the complete opposite. Although masculine in his own way he had flawless skin and deep-set eyes that made him look endearing and slightly feminine. The rainbow boa around his neck gave him SUPERSTAR and gay. But he was considered a fag, sweet and light in his loafers around the way. He was all of those things and more.

But he was also complicated love.

"Ajax..." he covered his mouth, fingertips brushing against his upper lips. "Who...who is this child? She's...she's the prettiest thing I've ever seen in my life."

Ajax grinned. "She's yours...for now..."

Lennon looked at him and then Kaysa. "But...how? I thought you said you didn't want a kid. I thought you said we couldn't afford one."

"I was wrong. I want you to have what you want so she's yours." Lennon rushed up to him and tried to kiss Ajax in gratitude but he backed away. "Just take the kid and love her while you can." He sighed. "Right now my feet hurt and I'm tired."

Normally Lennon would fight harder for affection despite knowing that the only place he showed him sexual attention was in the bedroom. But he also knew the devil he could become if poked. Unlike Lennon Ajax preferred to lie to the world about his sexuality, never revealing feelings for him in public. And yet, under the shield of sheets and the night sky he would assure Lennon that he was the only one while fucking him from behind.

Slowly Lennon took the child into his arms, examining a little closer everything about her he adored, even her weight. Always on, and loving the stares, Kaysa wrapped her arms around his neck and kissed his cheek. It was love at first sight for Lennon, a moment he would replay in his mind for years to come.

As he looked at the child, his heart exploding with love he said, "Where'd you get her?"

Ajax glared, his eyebrows pulling together. "Don't ever ask me that. She's yours now and that's all that matters."

"She's perfect, somebody has to love her," Lennon said gazing at her thick head of hair, yellow skin and rosy cheeks.

"It don't matter. You'll love her harder than her mother ever could."

"With all my heart."

"Don't forget our arrangement. I let you keep the kid and you make sure she's worth it when it's time."

Lennon nodded. "Yes...I...I remember, Ajax." He took a deep breath. "Just let me have her to myself at first, okay? And I'll make sure she's ready for you when the time is right."

"Keep your head in the game is all I'm saying." He pointed at him. "So what you gonna call it?" Ajax walked away and plopped on the side of the bed to remove his boots.

Lennon on the other hand took in Kaysa's features a bit closer as he pondered the question. For some reason he remembered his favorite aunt who died in a plane crash some years back and smiled. Since we're speaking of tales, she was also the baddest whore Baltimore had ever seen. A tall bitch, about 6'5" with firm titties the size of casaba melons and a mouth wetter than a pissy alley.

"I'm gonna call her Shayla...Shayla Bellard. After my auntie Cocaine Pussy." He nodded. "Yeah, that'll be her name and she'll be even better." He looked down at her. "Won't you?"

PART TWO

The WHORE The Wind Blew My Way

CHAPTER TWO

7 YEARS LATER

1983

Assorted feathers in a variety of colors were dusted against the hardwood floors in Ajax and Lennon's row home in Baltimore. While dancing, Lennon pirouetted around the living room in a red pair of women's underwear and a rainbow boa around his neck. Next to him was Shayla in her Super Woman pajama set, a red boa dripping over her shoulders. Wearing Lennon's large black high heel shoes she flopped around like she hadn't walked a day in her life, trying to keep up with her idol.

Although someone with a loud stereo system outside of their building could be heard blasting the 80's favorite Ladies Night by Kool & The Gang, they were watching *Mahogany* for the fiftieth time and Diana Ross was being photographed in Italy in the middle of a highway.

Shayla's eyes twinkled as she watched the dark skinned woman being hounded by paparazzi but above all she wanted the love between Diana and Billy

Dee. Movies were everything for Lennon and Shayla and they would escape into the lives of the actors and actresses to become anything other than what they were. Lennon, a male prostitute and Shayla a little girl who was told daily that in a little while she would become a woman.

"Move your hips, Shayla," Lennon instructed as he tossed his boa around, more feathers floating to the floor with every motion. "Throw your arms and hips from left to right. You must become Diana Ross!" He said playfully, a smile on his face.

"Like this, Dad-Ma?" She said shaking her hips like a child trying too hard.

He covered his mouth and laughed hysterically. She looked adorable and as far away from a woman as possible, but she was still his baby. "Just like that, Shayla. You're perfect."

"I can do more! Watch!" She spun around quickly and hit the floor in a hot messy fall. Her left knee was scraped, a little blood oozing outward. Seeing the wound, which looked worse than it felt, she cried hard and heavy.

Lennon tossed the boa down, picked her up and sat her on his lap on the sofa. "No crying, princess." He wiped her thick curly hair backward. "When you're a star nobody cares how you feel. It's all about how you make them feel and you have to remember that, always."

"Okay," She said, her lips poking outward. "But it hurts so—"

"What did I just tell you?"

She wiped her tears with her fists. "Nobody cares."

"I'm sorry."

"Nobody but me but never show emotion." He pointed at her face. "I don't want you to be shocked when the world shows you what I'm saying is true. That time is coming for sure. Tuck your emotions away, Shayla. Always—"

The door flew open. "He's on his way." Ajax entered the living room. He dusted invisible particles off his new black silk blouse, his natural smooth black hair pulled into a ponytail that dangled down his back. He definitely took the pimp persona to the highest-level possible when it came to his fancy clothing and rings on every available finger. "Get her dressed." He pointed at Lennon with his long fingernail.

Lennon sat Shayla on the sofa and stood up. Approaching him carefully he said, "Honey, can we, can we do this tomorrow? I mean...it's too early don't you think? She's only eight."

He frowned, eyes piercing into his soul, causing Lennon's legs to tremble. "I told you what the situation was when we first got her." He pointed his stiff nail into his chest. "And what did you say?"

"I know...it's just uh—"

"Don't fuck with me!" He fastened his gold cuff link. "Don't fuck with me, ever. Now get her dressed. You wasting time." He walked toward Shayla on the sofa, lowered down and looked at her. With a fake grin plastered on his face he said, "You're ready aren't you, big girl? You ready to become a woman today?"

She didn't answer.

He frowned, stood up and glared at Lennon. "The kid's acting like a bitch because you spoiling her. And that's gonna be a problem later." He paused. "Get the little ho dressed." He walked out of the house.

Unhurriedly, Lennon approached her. "Shayla, remember when I told you that soon you would have to play grown up? And that men would come visit you because you're so pretty?"

Shayla pushed her soft black hair from her face. "Yes...I remember."

"Well today is the day." He paused and tried to force the tears away. He loved this child more than himself but there was nothing he could do about it because Ajax was in charge.

Yes he was a whore, who had to give himself to Ajax and to any man who paid, but when it came to her he wanted to preserve her innocence as long as possible and even her virtue was out of his hands. In his mind she belonged to him. She was his child.

"What I gotta do to the man?"

"Sit on his lap and smile at him. Kiss him if he wants to and let him touch you. Okay?"

KNOCK. KNOCK. KNOCK.

He lifted her up, pulled off her clothes and threw on a red dress he picked out earlier that sat on the sofa. Next he grabbed his lavender robe off the chair and placed it on himself. When he was done he sprayed some perfume on her neck all while the knocks rapped against the door harder.

When he was done he looked down at her. "No matter how he makes you feel remember you're a star and stars never cry." He walked to the door opened it and Herbert Wilder stood on the outside. He was a thick biracial man with hooded eyes and hairy fingers. He was also a severe freak.

"'Bout time!" He said glaring at Lennon. "He took my money and I thought you were about to fuck with me."

"No...uh...I was getting her dressed." He paused. "Sorry it took so long. Please, come in."

He was irritated but his eyes brightened when he took in Shayla's untouched beauty. Her natural black hair ran down her back and her Asian eyes against her light brown skin made her look tropical. He strode toward the sofa and sat down. With an extended hand he said to Shayla, "Come here."

She didn't move.

Her limbs were stiff because something deep inside told her he would take everything she loved about life away, and she wanted to cherish happiness forever.

He was scary.

So she looked up at Lennon, wanting him to say she didn't have to go. Wanting him to say anything to make the strange man go away. "Dad-Ma..." Her lip trembled. "I'm sleepy. Can I take a nap?"

"Baby, you hate naps," he said softly. Lennon cleared his throat and clasped his hands in front of him. "Go to him, Shayla. Go to the nice man. Now!"

Head hung low, without another word, she crawled over to him and he whisked her up. Herbert looked up at Lennon. "Can we be alone?"

Lennon stepped closer with authority. "You are not to enter her. You know that—"

"I know the rules," he spat. "Now Ajax said we could be alone so I'm demanding that you leave."

Lennon looked down at Shayla wanting to take her away but there were many reasons he could not. For starters he wasn't strong enough mentally. His entire life had been Ajax and he never knew anything else.

Not only that but where would he take her? And what would their lives be like? When he realized alone he could not afford to take care of a child his heart ruptured deeper. He was as worthless as a shitty pamper. But the worse reason of all he would remain under Ajax's power was because he loved every mean, deceitful bone in his body.

"Yes...I'll...I'll give you some privacy." Slowly he walked into the bedroom but left it cracked slightly to watch.

Quickly, Herbert dug into his pants so that his penis was out but lying sideways on top of his slacks. When he was situated he placed Shayla on his lap and rocked her slowly back and forth over the growing hump. She could feel him stiffening under her body and so she closed her eyes.

In her mind, in that moment, she was Shirley Temple. As he kissed her face she thought about lights and cameras on her and she smiled. Suddenly the creep wasn't a stumpy man wanting to do dirty things to little girls. He was Billy Dee and she was Diana Ross. And suddenly, with a little mental work, her world wasn't as rough anymore.

Herbert, believing he was alone was about to take advantage of the child by raping her anyway when suddenly he was struck on the back of the head with a cast iron pan. With his scalp busted open Lennon yanked her up and ran her toward the door. With her tucked under one of his arms he rushed out and down the steps barefoot. He would get shoes later but for now it was time to go.

"Fuck this shit, nobody's touching my baby!" He ran out into the night. "Nobody!"

1 MONTH LATER

It had been one month since Lennon took Shayla from the apartment he shared with Ajax. He ascertained from the hood that he was looking for him and many times he thought about returning and taking the beating he knew would come his way. But he had Shayla and was afraid of what would happen to her if he allowed him to sell her so young.

But three things plagued him most of all. First he was broke, secondly he had a heroin habit, which caused him to mismanage money and lastly his heart still throbbed for Ajax.

Hungry, Lennon parked Shayla in the grocery cart and pushed her through the aisle. Shayla was wearing a huge green coat, which seemed out of season for the beautiful spring weather Baltimore had. The coat wasn't to keep her warm, but to stuff cans of ravioli into her pockets.

Grief took over Lennon's disposition as he realized he was using his little girl to steal but he would do all he could to take care of her, including breaking the law.

"Dad-Ma, I gotta pee." Shayla pressed her fingers between her legs and jiggled her foot in an attempt to control the tingling sensation. Her eyebrows rose with fear because she felt the urine coming at any moment. "Really, really bad. Can we go to the bathroom?"

"Hold it just a little bit longer okay?" Lennon looked around for security guards as he continued to push the cart down the aisle. When he realized the coast was clear he stuffed a can of ravioli into her jacket. "I'll take you to the toilet the moment we —"

"Who's that little girl?" A regal woman asked walking behind Lennon. She wore a grey business suit and sharp high heel shoes and it was as if she stepped out of a page in Ebony Magazine. She was also beautiful, with skin the color of dark bark. Although striking, her energy was harsh and firm and it put Lennon at immediate attention.

"What business is it of yours? Who are you?"

"What is her name?" She pointed at Shayla and waited for an answer. Her stance was as solid as a brick building and it was obvious she was going nowhere without a reply. "I asked who is she?"

Lennon frowned. He didn't recognize the woman or felt he owed her an explanation. He cleared his throat and said, "She's my daughter. Why?"

"You're lying!" She pointed at the air with stiff jabbing motions. "That's my little girl! I know my child when I see her and she was stolen from me years ago! In New York! They told me she may have died and I moved here! But what are you doing with her? Give her to me!" She moved toward him and he pushed her backward.

"Lady, you better get out of my face before I slice you!"

Shayla stood in horror as she watched the beautiful woman declare her as her own. Up until that instant she never thought about having a mother because she didn't know what one meant in the theoretical sense. She wasn't in school and every waking moment was spent with Lennon pretending to be anything other than who he was. This isolation put her out of touch with reality. Sure she'd seen mothers on TV but she considered everything on the tube to be make believe...even moms.

Lennon was an emotional wreck. The breath was knocked from his body with Louise's words because he knew she was probably right. So many years had fled that he never once considered anybody would find the little girl much less want her back. He even prayed if someone did want her returned they stopped hoping long ago, believing there wasn't another human alive who could give her more love. Not only that but Ajax never talked about where Shayla came from so he didn't know where to hide.

"I want my daughter," the woman cried. "Give her to me! Please!"

"You better get out of my face, bitch! I'm warning you!" Lennon yelled waving a fist in her direction. "This is my child and I'm not about to sit here and listen to you. And if you try to take her from me I will kill you."

"COPS! COPS! HELP! PLEASE!" Louise screamed at the top of her lungs, trying to remove Shayla from his grasp. "HELP ME! HE HAS MY BABY! HE HAS MY DAUGHTER!"

Lennon shoved Louise harder and she crashed into a display of canned green beans. Afterwards he yanked Shayla out of the cart and dashed out of the store, an angry mob behind him.

Lennon sped down the highway and didn't slow down until he was as far away from the grocery store as possible. Sweat poured down his forehead as if he'd been running the entire time. He didn't even stop completely until he could feel Shayla's large eyes peering at him. Taking a quick glance downward he saw pee dripping down Ajax's leather car seat. She had urinated everywhere.

When he saw a rest stop off Interstate 95 he pulled over and looked at her. "I'm sorry, Shayla." He took a deep breath. "I —"

"Who was that lady?" Her eyes were wide and hopeful. "Is she my mommy?"

SLAP! SLAP! SLAP!

He struck her three times and she held onto her warm face in disbelief. Glaring he said, "Don't look so scared. I get slapped all the time."

"Okay. I'm…I'm sorry."

He took a deep breath. "Now…I am your mother, your father and your caregiver! And if you ever call another woman mama again I will abandon you. Forever! Is that what you want?"

"No...no, Dad-Ma!" She crawled onto his lap, dampening his jeans but he didn't care. "I'm sorry. I'm sorry. Please don't leave me."

Lennon's thumping heart didn't slacken until he held her into his arms and rocked her softly. All of his life he wanted a family and he would go to jail before he gave her up, even to her own mother.

Separating from her he said, "I'm not going to leave you but we have to work together now. Do you know what that means?"

She shook her head no.

"It means doing things we don't wanna. But you have to trust me." He paused. "If you trust me I'll never let you down."

"Okay. I won't Dad-Ma."

At the end of the day there was only one thing he could do. He had to go back to the man who could keep both of them safe and accept his fate.

With his tail tucked, Lennon moped into the house he shared with Ajax holding his khaki colored suitcase in one hand and Shayla's fingertips in the other. Slowly Ajax rose off the sofa, walked over to them and smiled. On the floor model television, a commercial for Care Free Curl played softly and Shayla chose to focus on it, instead of whatever would be happening next.

Snaking his hand to the back of Lennon's neck, he pulled his face toward his and kissed Lennon on the forehead. Afterwards, he lifted Shayla off her feet, hugged her and looked into her eyes. The smell of urine in the air. "Are you okay?"

She nodded. "Yes, sir. Just hungry."

He placed her back down. "I'm gonna put some fries and fish sticks on for you later. Now go to your room. I have to talk to your dad-ma." Shayla walked slowly to the door, turning around once to look at Lennon before closing the door behind her self.

Curious about what would happen next, Shayla placed her ear against the cool panel and within seconds she heard a thud followed by Lennon's gasp. For five minutes there was soft whimpering followed by several more clunky sounds.

Despite being in severe pain Lennon wanted nothing more than to make sure Shayla didn't hear his cries. He knew she was afraid and hearing him being beaten might put her further on edge.

"Please," Lennon whispered after his body weakened. "I...I can't take anymore."

Ajax was merciless. In the end he had beaten Lennon so badly, he was unconscious for the rest of the day.

Ajax made his stance clear to all.

After what happened to Lennon, Shayla knew she would never be able to escape because he also owned her soul.

CHAPTER THREE

SHAYLA

1988

Lennon stood on his knees in front of Shayla who was sitting on a chair in her bedroom. The radio was on and *Greatest Love Of All* by *Whitney Houston* played quietly in the background. He hummed a little as he placed a mirage of makeup on her face ranging from hot pink for her cheeks to turquoise for her eyelids.

Thirteen-year old Shayla reached up and touched his lightly bruised face. "Does it still hurt?" Time may have passed but the whippings didn't and there were signs from a recent beating around his eyes. As a result Lennon's usual vibrant personality was mellowed which only worsened when he was high.

Lennon smiled. "The pain is gone there." He pointed at his eyes. "But still hurts here." He pointed at his heart. "But I'll be okay. I always am."

When Shayla's makeup was done he propped a synthetic, itchy, gold wig on her head and took a deep breath. After fighting and making up with Ajax for five years, he managed to prevent Shayla from losing her virginity to prostitution. And now the fight was over.

Ajax made it clear that either she earned her keep like the two other girls he had on the stroll or he would kill her. Lennon knew the inevitable had finally come. She was thirteen and it was time to get down to business. Besides, he had started much earlier.

"Who are you?" He asked looking at her painted face.

She batted her eyes and winked. "Marilyn Monroe."

"Great choice, darling," he smiled. "In which movie?"

"Uh…Gentlemen Prefer Blondes."

He smiled and fluffed her wig, a single tear treaded down his cheek. She immediately noticed. "Why you crying?"

He wiped his tear away roughly. "Because it's going to hurt badly, Shayla. I ain't never been in the business of lying to you and I'm sure not about to start now." He sniffled and wiped more tears away. "And I want you to be prepared for it because it may be the most painful thing you've experienced in your life."

"Harder than The Wand?"

In the past Lennon had taken to inserting the portion of a broken pool stick inside of her to end her virginity, which he called The Wand, saying it changed little girls into women. He smoothed one side with sand paper but the other side, which had a rounded shape that he placed a condom on to widen her space a little at a time instead of all at once.

"A little harder but it won't feel good."

Shayla took a deep breath. "I'll be fine. At least Ajax won't hurt you anymore because you don't want me to go." She paused. "Plus I'm thirteen and —"

He grabbed both sides of her face and pulled her toward him. "Close your eyes, baby. You close your eyes and go elsewhere in your mind. Don't let him take your peace from you because you have to dig deep to find it. And —"

KNOCK. KNOCK. KNOCK.

"Lennon, open up, Shayla's visitor is here," Ajax said authoritatively on the other side of the door. "Let's not waste anymore time getting her prettier than what she already is." He paused. "You ready in there, baby girl?"

"Yes." She nodded.

"Okay, Ajax, just give me a few more —"

"OPEN THIS FUCKING DOOR!" Ajax yelled. "NOW!"

Lennon walked Shayla to the bed and laid her down. "Remember what I said. Close your eyes tightly, Shayla," he whispered. "Go someplace nice from one of our movies." He paused. "I love you and I hope some day you can forgive me."

When Lennon opened the door Ajax grabbed him in the back of the neck and tossed him into the hallway, allowing Herbert to enter the room. Ajax turned to Herbert and said, "Whatever you do don't hurt her face! Leave her pretty like you found her!"

Herbert grinned and licked his lips. Never liking Lennon after he split open his head with a pan.

He wanted revenge.

"I won't touch a hair on her head." He grabbed the knob and closed the door. Next he walked over to the small radio and knocked it to the floor, to cease its sound. Eyes stone with disgust, Herbert undressed at the foot of the bed as Shayla hid under the covers, only her eyes peeking through. First he removed his pants, then his cream boxers before stroking himself in front of her. "You scared, girl?"

"No," she lied. "I'm fine."

"Good, 'cause I'm gonna be easy with you." He sucked his teeth. "You want me to be easy don't you?"

"Yes, I do." She closed her eyes and thought about the song 'Diamonds Are A Girl's Best Friend'. She hummed the words repeatedly until she felt him get on top of her, push her legs apart and enter her vagina like he was trying to hammer a nail into a piece of wood.

The pain was so excruciating her eyes flew open and she cried out in agony, wanting nothing more than for him to stop. Lennon, hearing her voice, banged on the door in an attempt to help. "Is she okay in there?"

"What I tell you about fucking up my money?" Ajax could be heard before hitting Lennon in the stomach. "She's a woman now! You can't stop her!"

Shayla continued to cry until Herbert slammed his hand over her mouth and looked down at her. "I waited for you long enough, bitch." He paused. "Now you will shut up or else I will give you something to cry about!" He pressed harder. "And trust, I've done it before. Do you understand me?"

She nodded, closed her eyes again and submitted to being raped. And instead of escaping in her mind like she had in the past, she was there for every agonizing moment.

Lennon wept on the dining room floor after hearing Shayla's painful voice from inside her room. Annoyed as fuck, slowly Ajax squatted next to him. "You love her more than me don't you?" He paused. "Don't you?"

Lennon shook his head from left to right so quickly he got a little dizzy. "What are you talking about? Of course I don't love her more. How else could you convince me to let you do this? When you know how much I cared."

"Let you do this?" He frowned. "Bitch, are you crazy? You really do think you have a say so in all of this don't you?" He paused. "When I brought that red ho to you I told you what would happen. You even convinced me to keep her pure up until this moment which was good because he paid top money for her just now." He pointed at the door. "But you never was supposed to put her before me. Ever!"

"But I don't."

"You do! And if you want to survive, if you want to live you better remember who I am. The owner of all I perceive!"

CHAPTER FOUR

THREE MONTHS LATER

Shayla was watching *Weird Science* in the living room with Lennon while waiting on her next 'Visitor', which was code for another man paying for sex with a minor. Ajax had made lots of money from Shayla and she had quickly become the best of the four young prostitutes on his roster. Because of her he bought a pink Cadillac, with crystals embedded in the dashboard and visor just to lure in more girls. Youngin's loved sparkling things.

When she giggled hard, Lennon smiled and looked over at her. "What you so happy about?"

She pointed at the TV because she was enamored at Kelly Le Brock who played Lisa. The way she had the young boys geeking over her in Shayla's opinion was fascinating. "Am I pretty like her, ma?" She asked Lennon, never taking her gaze off the screen.

"No." He said firmly.

Confused, her head rotated quickly toward him. "Huh? I'm not?"

"You're prettier." He grinned.

Shayla laughed and stood in front of the TV and placed her hands on her hips. Since she had watched the movie more than enough she even practiced her pouty mouth like her. "Do pretty girls get what they want, ma? If they're real pretty, can they still get hurt?"

He grinned again. "Nope. The world is your oyster."

The door opened and in walked Ajax with a twelve-year-old cute brown girl with thick black hair. She was holding a doll and it was evident that she'd been crying. Lennon approached them and Shayla stood next to him, gawking at the girl harder. This was the first time she'd seen a girl close to her age and she hoped she was staying.

"Ajax, who...who is she?" Lennon asked.

Ajax removed his leather gloves and tossed them on the table. "You know Angela, the dope head down the street right?"

Lennon nodded. "I do."

"Well she gave her to me. So we keeping her. Make her comfortable."

Lennon's eyes widened. "But we don't have any room for no more ho's." He paused. "It's tight in here already from the other girls who sleep over between shifts. We need a bigger place if we gonna be letting ho's lay their heads in our house."

"You under the impression your opinion matters to me. Get her cleaned up and ready for her first visitor, bitch. He's coming tonight."

Bernice was in the tub soaking when Shayla knocked on the door and walked inside. She sat on the floor next to the tub and looked at her, taking in all of her pretty features. "Have you had visitors before?"

"I don't know what that mean." Bernice wiped her tears away. "What they gonna do with me?"

Shayla shrugged. "Just stuff. "

"But what kind of stuff?"

"Nasty stuff."

Shayla thought about all the men she had and tried to wipe the thoughts from her mind but it didn't work. The bites on her neck, the rough sucks on her nipples to where they would throb for days at a time and also the anal entries. It was all madness. Who knows what kind of creep Bernice would have on her first day.

Instead of saying more she sang a nursery rhyme softly that Ajax had sang to her as a joke. *'Baa Baa black sheep have you any whores? Yes, sir, yes sir, three rooms full. Some for my master, some for my lames, some for the old men who live down the lane.'*

Bernice frowned. "What is that?"

Shayla shrugged. "Just a song Ajax taught me. It relaxes me sometimes. Sounds nice don't it?"

"Nah." She paused. "And I don't like him."

Shayla's eyes widened. "You can say that to me if you wanna," she whispered. "I'll even listen to it a few more times if you in the mood, but you can never let one of the other girls hear you say that. Especially the pretty one called Beverly outside. It could mean your life."

Bernice nodded, feeling more defeated.

"Do you like TV and movies?" Shayla asked with brightened eyes. "'Cause I do! I know all the lines to my favorites."

"Kinda, but we didn't get to watch much at my house. My mama sold the TV long ago. And when she didn't have nothing else to sell she sold me next. That's why I'm here."

"Well all you gotta do when the visitors come is think about your favorite star." Shayla looked into the ceiling. "And then—"

"I had one before," Bernice sniffled.

"One what?"

"A man. He put his fingers in me and scratched me so bad I thought I got my period. Blood was everywhere." She moved closer to the side of the tub so Shayla could hear her clearly. "It didn't feel good at all but he made me tell him it did."

"Want me to loosen you up?" She swallowed. "Like my Dad-Ma does to me sometimes?"

Bernice's eyes widened. "Will it hurt?"

"Not as bad as if you didn't get loosened up first."

"Okay," she sniffled again. "You can."

Shayla rushed over to the side of the toilet, grabbed a plunger with a wooden handle.

Bernice frowned. "Ewww...what's that?"

"Well my Dad-Ma used The Wand but Ajax threw it away, saying I didn't need it no more since I was already a woman. This will work though."

Shayla placed it next to the tub, took her clothes off and eased inside with Bernice. Next she grabbed the plunger, leaving the rubber part outward. "You gotta open your legs now."

Bernice's eyebrows rose. "But it's gonna…"

"I won't hurt you." Shayla said softly. "Promise."

Bernice widened her legs and doing what Lennon had done to her many times; Shayla placed the unsanitary tip of the plunger handle inside her vagina softly. The water provided some lubricant but not much. Although it didn't go all the way in Bernice still squinted in pain. Oddly enough, the agony she felt was nothing compared to the mad man that would take advantage of Bernice later that night and the night after that.

This moment began the sister hood, that they would share for a long dark, time.

Sitting at the kitchen table, Lennon had another black eye and a bag of heroin as his reward. Every time

Ajax hit him he would buy him drugs knowing it would make him easily forget. After all, heroin was a painkiller.

The mental games Ajax would play with Lennon happened for a reason. Over time Lennon had developed a bond with all of the girls so that when he was hurt, the girls functioned at a lower level. So it was important to keep Lennon high or happy, either one was okay with him. Sure Ajax could beat his girls into submission, which he did anyway if he had time on his hands, but he preferred to fake love to make his pimp game more effective.

They were sitting in the kitchen when Shayla asked, "Do you love him?"

Lennon's eyes remained on the spoon and the heroin he was placing on top of it. "Love who, baby? What you talking 'bout now? And did you clean your room for your next visitor?"

"Yes and I'm talking about Ajax. Do you love him?"

Finally he looked up at her. "Very much."

"More than you love me?"

"More than I love myself, Shayla. I'm sorry but I pray you never love a man that hard."

She swallowed. "Well I'm gonna have a special love too one day. One like on TV because I'm pretty and I know how to make a man feel good. They tell me all the time."

"You can have whatever you want." He focused on the dope and the spoon. "You most certainly can." He nodded at her and ran heat under the spoon, watching it bubble. "That you can be sure of." He was just talking shit but she was eating it up.

Shayla giggled. "And when he finds me he's gonna take me away from it all," she smiled before twirling around. "Away from Ajax and this place. Watch! It's gonna happen. I been praying on it."

Lennon put the spoon down, stood up and slapped her to the floor. Next he looked behind her at the door to be sure no one was coming. For the moment he resembled Ajax. "How you sound? Talking all crazy and stuff?" He pointed at her. "You never leaving this place and you never leaving me." He grabbed her arms. "Do you hear me?"

She nodded as thick tears rolled down her face. "You all I got in this world, Shayla. Dreams are just that...dreams. They ain't meant to alter real life or change things in the present. Don't be foolish when you talking."

"What about Bernice?"

"What about her?" He sat down.

"You say I'm all you got. But what about her?" She pointed to the closed door where Bernice lay behind it with a man.

"She Ajax's problem." He grabbed his heroin and ran the fire under the spoon. "But you mine and it's gonna stay that way." He paused and dipped the needle into the dope. "And you know why?"

"No..."

"Because a devil gotta have souls to rule his kingdom. And ours belong to Ajax." He shot the dope into his vein and drifted into ecstasy. "They sho do."

CHAPTER FIVE

SHAYLA

1993

With the money made with Ajax's girls, Ajax was able to purchase a four-story row house in Baltimore City. The brick property was taken care of well by the landscapers and from the outside it looked like just another cozy home in the fledging neighborhood with one exception, they were selling pussy behind the walls.

Plenty of it.

Out of the other eight bedrooms in the house, Shayla's was the most glamorous. Not only was it bigger but it also smelled nicer than the others. The mixture of fresh lavender and jasmine was a welcoming treat in her abode as opposed to the raw pussy odor steaming from the girls who didn't wash between clients, or even when the night ended for that matter.

After being led to Shayla's room by one of the whore's twelve-year old daughter, the visitor, Frankie, stood in awe, as he watched her lie sideways on the bed gazing at him seductively. A music connoisseur at heart, Shayla had the radio on as *H-town's* song *Knockin The Boots* played softly from its speakers.

With years under her belt, having sex with Shayla was now an experience. A professional through and through she had been called *Cocaine Pussy*, after her namesake, also Lennon's aunt.

The John, a slender black man with an extra large belly stood in the doorway and said, "You so pretty…" He closed the door.

"Why thank you." Shayla's blonde wig, fake diamond jewelry and soft white lingerie made her look like a light skin Marilyn Monroe with Asian flare of course. "Well how you doing, big fella? You ready for me?

"You bet I am, superstar," he said removing his tie. "I'm going to eat you alive." His eyes widened and his hand extended believing he might have offended her. "I'm sorry…I…guess I forgot my manners. I didn't mean I would really eat you."

She smiled and then winked, having caught his awe. She mastered the art of seduction long ago. And now at the tender age of eighteen she was straight biz.

"Don't worry about all that, handsome." She stood on her knees on the bed. "Now are you gonna stand at attention the entire night or come on over here with me so I can make your dreams come true? I prefer the latter."

His dick stiffened and he licked his lips as he listened to her voice. Part of him wanted to play the job of a spectator because it was usually difficult to get her. Just looking at her physique got him aroused. Luckily for his penis someone cancelled and he got her after his first request. "I'm gonna come over there." Quickly he removed his clothes and rushed over to the mattress.

After sliding his body in the center of the bed, face up, he raised her by the hips and placed her on top of him, although he hadn't entered her yet. "Shayla, I —" She covered his lips with her index finger.

"Marilyn, baby. My friends call me Marilyn and if you want, you can do the same."

He heard she enjoyed role-play and that was part of the reason he wanted her services. From the white leather furniture in her room, the huge pictures of Marilyn Monroe, Audrey Hepburn, Bettie Davis, Diana Ross and Diahann Carroll on the wall, he felt as if he were in the room of a young starlet.

"Marilyn, you're the most beautiful—"

She kissed his face and grabbed a condom stopping his words. "Monroe, baby. Marilyn Monroe." Her eyes widened as she waited for him to fulfill her request. "Say my name, daddy." She removed his penis and stroked him until he stiffened. When he looked down the condom was on and he didn't even know she opened it let alone slipped it on his pole. Slowly she placed his dick into her body and eased on top of him. "Mmmmmm, that feels right...now say my name."

His mouth opened but words failed to exit fully. He was in a different world. Her pussy felt like a hand massage and he was blown away. The stories were all right. "Marilyn...Monroe." The name leveled on one long breath. "Marilyn Monroe."

She winked and rode him softly at first before quickening her pace, her ass flapping up and down like a flag sideways. "That's my baby." Fingers pressed into the grooves of his chest she propelled faster, turning her body into waves on an ocean. "Say it again."

"Marilyn."

She bit her bottom lip and relished the power she exalted over him. During this time in her life she enjoyed sex. She had to. It was necessary for her to escape the world and some men handled her better than others. Since a role model was out of the question she gauged her happiness by the satisfaction of the men in her bed.

If they were good she was great.

"Give me that dick, daddy," she moaned. "Give it to Marilyn hard, long and fast."

"You, you want this dick?" His breath was short, quick and choppy. "You ready for it?"

"I want it badder than anything I ever have in my life." She moved up and down. "Badly...please don't make me wait. I wanna feel that cum gush inside of me. I wanna feel it now."

Shayla rocked and swooped on this nigga's dick until he exploded into the condom. In all of his life he had never been fucked like that and he doubted he ever would again.

Tired and sweaty, he placed his hands on her waist and said, "Let me take you away from here. You name the place and we'll go."

Her jaw hung open. "Really? Are you...are you sure?"

He grabbed her face and looked up into her eyes. "You better than this place. Let me take you out of here and show you the world. Use the globe as your resource because there is no limit. I have all the money we need."

"But I have Bernice." She thought about her sister who was in a room not too far from hers, having sex with her visitor. "She'd never be able to make it without me. I must take her too if we gonna go."

"Well bring her with us." He paused. "I realize you don't know me but you will learn to love me, Marilyn. I promise you."

She smiled and looked down at him, considering him closely. He was a little heavier than she liked her beaus and of course she didn't love him. It could also be said that he wasn't the type of man she could see forever with but after fixing him up a little, with is money of course, she was sure she could make him like the actors on TV.

"When?" She said excitedly. "I'm ready now if you wanna leave. I just have to get Bernice ready?"

"Cool, I'll be back tomorrow. But you have to put me on the list because it's hard to see you."

She nodded. "I'll run a little later with one of my clients so that I can make time for you. Even if you call and they tell you I'm booked come anyway and ask for me. I'll be waiting."

Bernice paced her dark, dirty room in a frantic haze upon talking to her sister. Shayla had just whispered something to her that was reminiscent of saying Bloody Mary three times in the mirror, in the dark. If even one of the whores overheard them it could mean their lives.

As Shayla stood before her sister she thought of something. It was actually sad. Their rooms were as different as night and day. Her's smelled of old sex and crabs that Bernice tried to cover up with cheap perfume. This deed only made the stench worse and caused her nostril hairs to thicken. But no matter what Shayla loved her, beyond words and their bond had only solidified as the calendar years turned.

"I don't wanna leave daddy, Shayla," she scratched her woolly uncombed hair. "I don't wanna leave Lennon either. What if, what if we go out in the world and we can't take care of ourselves? I don't wanna be on the streets. Jamie just came back after being gone two weeks and she was almost killed."

Shayla moved closer. "That's 'cause she went to a frat party with fifteen men alone." Shayla grabbed her gritty hands. "Don't you see? If we leave with him we'll be together. That's different. We got each other."

The door opened and Beverly appeared. She was a tall brown skin girl who made the best wigs and so her hair always looked natural and expensive. I'm talking thick luscious flowing curls. Standing at the door she wore tight blue jeans and a pink top and a face of evil. "What ya'll in here talking about?"

Bernice hid behind Shayla. "Nothing..."

"That ain't what I heard just now," Beverly said twirling one of her curls around her finger. Next she sniffed the air hard. "Wow, after all this time you still don't know how to wash your pussy, Bernice." She looked at Shayla. "You'd think Miss Superstar over here would show you. I guess she's selfish as always."

Shayla stepped closer. "Get out! NOW!"

Beverly's eyes widened and Shayla moved closer.

"I said get out!" Shayla continued.

Beverly backed into the hallway and ran away. Shayla closed the door again and approached Bernice. "You shouldn't have done that, Shayla." She said anxiously. "She's gonna tell him I know it."

"Fuck her," she smiled. "It doesn't matter anymore. We're leaving. Dad-Ma will understand and Ajax will get over it. Besides, he has Beverly. What he want with me?"

"I'm afraid..."

"Please, Berny I need you. I can't do this alone. It's our last chance to have a real life." She smiled. "You may even meet a man and if the guy doesn't work out we'll save enough money and move together. We can do this."

Her eyes widened. "For real? Do you really think I can find someone, even if I don't...look like..." she touched Shayla's cheek. "You?"

Shayla frowned. "You sound crazy! You're prettier than me, Berny. Way prettier." She hugged her again. "Don't you wanna have fun? Don't you wanna see the world outside of here? Let's do this."

She nodded. "Okay."

By T. Styles   127

She clapped her hands together. "Great, then we leaving tomorrow at—"

Suddenly, Ajax kicked the door open. He had a bloody white hand towel in his grasp and he was wiping his fingers and rings. "What yah in here doing?" He looked around. "'Cause it damn sure ain't sucking dicks."

"Nothing," Bernice said shaking her head. "Just talking with Shayla is all." She looked at her. "Ain't that right?"

"Well how come Beverly ran out of here crying?" He looked at Bernice. "You fucking with one of my top bitches?"

"No...I—"

"Get your funky ass up and get ready," he yelled at her. "You got a visitor willing to pay for trash pussy and I can't have my money fucked with. MOVE HO!"

CHAPTER SIX

SHAYLA

In her bedroom, Shayla had just finished having sex with Frankie and she was breathing heavily trying to slow her heart rate. Looking down at him, his dick still inside of her body she grinned. "I love how we feel together. It's so...so...perfect."

He rubbed her back and then gripped her waist. "Me too. I never had a woman get me there like you. Ever."

"Good...cause I'm ready to go with you." Shayla looked behind herself and then back at him. "Bernice is ready too. The sooner the better so nobody will find out."

He winked. "Was hoping you'd say that."

"So where you gonna take us?"

He grinned and placed both hands behind his head. "To this beautiful little cottage I have off the shore of Virginia Beach. The view is spectacular, Marilyn and we gonna have the best life there. I promise you. I have a maid who will cook anything you desire and make sure the house is always clean.

All you gotta do is look pretty and make love to me. I know you can handle that. Right?"

"You know I can." Shayla rose up and his limp dick fell out of her body. She sat next to him, looked at the door and back at him. "I don't care where we go but we have to be careful. Ajax is a really mean man. So what you have to do is pull around back when you leave so that he doesn't see you and — "

He chuckled once. "Wait, you're not serious are you?"

Her eyes widened. "What you talking about?"

"You're still acting right? Role playing like they told me you like to do?"

"Frankie, I...I..." Her jaw opened and closed. "What...what are you talking about?"

He rose off the bed and grabbed his pants. "Marilyn, Shayla or whatever your fucking name is I'm not about to take a whore out in public. I was just playing with you the other day, so that it would be good for our sex life. You know that right? I thought it was what you wanted."

She was devastated and her stomach bubbled. "But I...my sister...I told her...I told her you were saving us."

He shook his head. "Well maybe you shouldn't have." He grabbed his shirt and slipped it on. "Like I said, I thought you were playing. You wanted me to call you Marilyn Monroe and said your sister's name was Bernice, just like the real Marilyn Monroe. I thought this was all a game."

"But...you, you said you love me." Her belly rumbled and her breaths were short and sporadic. "Why would you lie like this? Why play games?"

"Don't blame me! You wanted to hear those words!" He yelled pointing at the floor. "Now I'm a happily married man. I have people who rely on me who need me to be there for them. I'm not going anyplace with you."

"But what were all of those things you were saying? You made me think that you wanted me. That you..."

He stormed toward the door, turned the knob and opened it because the young bitch had him fucked up. Before walking out he stopped short and said, "Don't get me wrong, your pussy is good. Really good. But who would really want you as a wife? You used up. I think you forgot that." He walked out.

Shayla was devastated.

So devastated a small amount of urine escaped her body and released onto her sheets. In less than 24 hours she had allowed a stranger to sell her a future and she paid for it with her heart and soul. Now it was all over.

With tears rolling down her cheek she rushed out of bed. Time was not on her side. She had to tell Bernice not to pack and to be careful. How foolish she felt about making her believe in the lie also knowing she would follow her lead.

She was at the door when Ajax came flying inside. "Hi...Ajax...I was just about to — "

The moment she opened her mouth he stole her in the face with a closed fist. Her lips busted open. Knuckles dripping with her blood he said, "Open your mouth, bitch!"

"Daddy, please don't. I — "

"OPEN YOUR FUCKING MOUTH!"

Slowly she widened her jaws and he said, "Lick the blood off my hand. Clean."

Her tongue ran alongside his knuckles as she tasted her own salty liquid. Tears continue to roll down her face and as she did when she was a child, she tried to imagine she was another person, in a magical place. In this world she was happy and cherished but with Ajax gripping her hair so hard the roots stung she was blasted back into reality.

"You think these niggas you be fucking want you gone?" He questioned. "Do you? How else they gonna get a hold of you?"

"I don't know," she sobbed harder. "But I'm so sorry. I'm so sorry."

"They don't want you gone because they need access to you and they get it by you staying here." He gripped her hair harder. "Ain't nobody taking your ho ass out this house. You will never leave …do you understand me? EVER!"

"Yes," she wept. "I understand."

He released her. "Good, now go clean your funky pussy and get ready for your next client. Don't play me!" He walked out the room.

On the floor, by the door she said, "But how long do you think I'll let you keep me here?" She stood up and walked slowly to the bed before flopping down and sobbing uncontrollably.

Normally she took pride in her body and would shower after each man instead of washing her vagina in the sink like most whores. But today she didn't care.

She lay sideways on the damp urine and cum soaked bed and within seconds Bernice came rushing into the room and up to the mattress.

Crawling up behind Shayla she stroked her arm softly. Her skin smelled unclean and stale but it was the love she felt when Bernice was around that comforted her. "It was Beverly who told him about us escaping," she whispered. "I know it."

"It doesn't matter if she did say anything," she exhaled. "He was lying to me anyway. Just playing with my mind and that shit hurts so bad. How could I be so stupid?"

Bernice wiped her hair. "Don't worry, one day you and me gonna find somebody who loves us. And when they do it won't be nothing daddy can do about it."

"Well I hope it happens soon, Bernice because right now I feel like I can die. I'm just gonna die."

CHAPTER SEVEN

SHAYLA

When Oliver opened the door Shayla looked at him and forced a smile on her face. He was a tall white man with piercing blue eyes and he was wearing navy blue mechanic coveralls.

She'd seen so many men that day, that all she could do was lie still and let them do what they wanted to her body. With her heart broken by buying into the dream, her head was not in the business but for some reason she still held onto hope that someone, some day, would eventually take her from her bleak world.

"Hey, there," Oliver said, his pale skin reddening the more he took in the curves of her body as she lie sideways looking in his direction. "They…they told me to come up here. Is it a good time?"

"Of course." She smiled. "Come closer." She paused. "It's been a long day but I promise I have enough energy left for you."

He moved closer and stood in front of her. "I've…I've…I've never done anything like this before. I don't know how it's supposed to go down."

"It won't hurt, I promise."

"Oh yeah?" He chuckled. "They said you were pretty but they didn't do you justice. "You...you look like a...a...movie star." He gazed around her room at the pictures on the walls. "Better...better than these women you got posted up here. I'm serious."

She sat on her knees in bed and with both hands beckoned him. "What you want me to call you? During our time together?"

He looked down and then back into her eyes. "Oliver."

"Well, Oliver, what can I do for you? How can I make your troubles go away?"

"Why...why are you...why are you..." He stuffed his hands into his pockets. "You know what I'm trying to say."

"Do you mean why am I here?"

He nodded. "Yes."

"So you wanna talk?" She paused. "Is that it?"

"Only a little at first if you don't mind." He paused. "Just trying to figure you out. Not judging...just guessing."

"Well guess down here where it's more comfortable." She pulled his hand down and he sat on the edge of the bed. Taking a deep breath she said, "To answer your question I'm here because nobody has taken me away yet." She maneuvered his chin so that he was looking into her eyes. "Maybe you can. Since you're interested."

"How old are you?" He asked.

"Eighteen."

He wiped his sweaty hands on his pants because the anticipation was killing him. "He...he...said said you were fifteen. I think his name is Ajax."

"That's because when you pay I can be whatever you want me to be. In this room age is just a number you choose." She ran her thumb over his bottom lip and kissed it. "So what's your pleasure?"

His tongue flitted around in his mouth. "Eighteen is cool." He nodded.

"See, we getting along good already." She looked at the clock. "Now are you sure all you wanna do is talk? Because our time is running out and I'd hate for you to leave unsatisfied."

All of a sudden, as if he was slapped in the ass like a racehorse, he quickly undid his pants and stood in front of her naked from the waist down. "If...if you don't...don't mind...you can...you can sit on the edge of the bed and I'll do the rest."

"Sure thing, big fella." Figuring he wanted his dick sucked she opened her mouth and waited for his special delivery.

"That's okay, you don't have to do that. Just sitting right there is good enough."

He yanked on his limp penis and quickly rubbed it to a thickness. Without her help at that. She tried to look away to prevent his cum from getting into her eyes while at the same time be attentive to his needs. There he stood jerking off himself and within seconds white cream gushed out of his pink dick and sprayed all over her face.

She grabbed the edge of the sheet and wiped his sperm off her eyelids and nose. *That was quick.* She thought. Relieved he was done she stood up and prepared to wash her face when he blocked her path. "I'm...I'm sorry. But...but I paid for...for an hour and I'm not done yet."

"Oh...well...usually, most men leave when they cum."

"I know...but Ajax said I could have the whole hour and I'm just getting started."

When it was all said and done he jacked off in five areas of her body not entering her once. Still she felt more comfortable around him than the rest, although slightly grossed out at his need to jerk off instead of feel a woman. At least there was no pain.

Suddenly she had a plan.

After draining his own semen and with a little time on the clock, he lie face up on the bed next to her. His breaths were heavy, as if he'd run five races. "That…that was great." He moaned. "Thank you, Shayla."

"No problem. I enjoyed it too." Her head rolled toward him. "Can I trust you with a secret?"

He rubbed his stomach and his eyes remained closed. He was exhausted. "I…I don't see why not."

"What do you think of me?" She paused. "I mean seriously."

"You playing?"

"Nope."

"You're perfect. I know I didn't touch you but that never was my thing anyway. I can't feel what I'm fucking with a condom so I prefer to…you know…do it the other way." He paused. "It was no offense against you."

She was unconcerned with the fucking. She wanted out. "Well I don't want to be here anymore," she whispered. "My sister and I are being forced to live here and sleep with men we don't like. I need your help. Please."

His eyes widened. "But what can I do?"

"You can help get us out of here," she whispered. "You can take us with you. Even if you don't want to keep us forever, just give us a few days and I'll make it work."

He smiled. "You...you would stay with me? A complete stranger?"

"I'm with strangers now." She whispered. "I'd go in an instant. But my sister has to go too. That's the deal."

He frowned. "But why is that important?"

"Because she's family," she sighed. "And I would've left a long time ago if I didn't have her so I will not leave her behind. I hope you can understand." She paused. "Can I count on you? Please?"

Ajax stomped up to Shayla's room, pushed the door open and stomped inside. Oliver was standing in front of it, fastening his coveralls. He stood tall, as if he had all authority over the situation. "Hey, Ajax..."

"Your time up." Ajax told him looking at his watch. "And if you forget the rules again you won't be allowed back." He tried to walk around him but Oliver blocked his path by standing in his way.

"That's close enough."

From where Ajax stood he could see Shayla sitting on the bed, her back against the headboard, legs crossed at the ankles and hair damp due to showering. "What's going on, Shayla? I'm about to hurt this dude. Are you talking crazy to my customers again?"

"Oh...about her," Oliver said. "She's coming with me." He scratched the back of his head and crossed his arms over his chest.

Ajax frowned. "Fuck you mean she's coming with you?" He looked past him at Shayla. "Get up, girl, I have to talk to this nigga alone. And if you act fast I won't beat your ass next."

She ignored him.

"Ain't you listening? She doesn't want to talk, man." Oliver persisted. "Like I said, she's coming with me. I told you that already."

Ajax tried to rough his way inside but Oliver grew violent and shoved him so hard he flew into the wall in the hallway. His body print crashed into the wall leaving a huge dent in its structure. "You don't want war with me, Ajax," Oliver threatened. "Now this girl is being forced to —"

Ajax stood up, rushed him and slammed his brass knuckles into Oliver's right cheek destroying his facial features. Delirious, Oliver tumbled backward and Ajax climbed on top of him and beat him crazy as Shayla watched from the bed horrified by the entire scene.

What have I done? She thought to herself.

The massacre occurring was all her fault.

When he was unconscious Ajax rose and dragged him into her bedroom. Huffing and puffing, brass knuckles dripping with red fluid onto her floor, he stood at the foot of the bed. Without saying anything else, he beat Shayla into a stupor.

Dizzy and discombobulated, he flopped into a wooden chair in the corner of her room. She was bloody as he talked to her. "I have placed you on a pedestal for most of your life. That ends today." He pointed at the floor. "From here on out you will exchange rooms with Levisha and be given the most violent men. Let's see how you like that treatment. Since you got this nigga talking slick."

Bernice crept into Shayla's room and approached the bed, trying not to awake her if she was asleep. Her face was so swollen she couldn't open her eyes fully but she was definitely conscious. "Oh my god, Shayla," she sniffled upon seeing her face. "I'm so sorry. Look at what he did to you."

Trying to be strong, Bernice took a deep breath and rushed into the bathroom. She grabbed a bucket, warm water and soap. Filling up the bowl she reentered the room and wiped the blood off of her face, carefully and with a lot of love and attention.

"Dad says you'll be leaving here for Levisha's room," she whispered looking at the door. "You'll do well anywhere."

"I don't care."

Shayla nodded and rested her head in Bernice's lap as she stroked her hair. "Well let me give you a few pointers because her men are going to go crazy over you 'cause of how pretty you are and all."

"You pretty too, Bernice," she paused. "Don't let these bastards tell you something different because of your skin color. It's all stupid anyway."

Bernice nodded. "Okay...well, since you so pretty," she looked down at Shayla and rubbed her hair, "Like me...there are few things you have to know. First the toilet in her room backed up so she started peeing in the sink. Never go in there barefoot if you can help it because she don't tidy at all, even worse than me if you can believe it." She paused. "Plus all of her men like it rough. I'm talking hair pulling, really hard slapping and choking during blow jobs." Bernice looked into the room and a single tear rolled down her face. "But the worst of 'em all is Lyle." She looked down at Shayla. "Shayla, if you can avoid him please try your best. Do whatever you can because he's a monster. Maybe dad will let Levisha keep him since she's used to him and all."

"I'll try," she said in a soft whisper.

"Good," Bernice smiled. "Feels so strange me helping you but I like it. Seems like I'm one year older than you and not the other way around."

Shayla tried to smile but her face ached. "So who he giving my room too?"

"You ain't heard?"

"No."

"Beverly, and she been telling all the girls she the bottom ho now. I swear I can't trust that bitch! You shouldn't either."

CHAPTER EIGHT

SHAYLA

Levisha's room was barely inhabitable.

For starters the mattress was so thin it was like paper and there were so many bed bugs they had gathered in the bed, pockets of space within the light fixtures and even sockets. But none of the men she'd been forced to sleep with seemed to care.

They were plain old nasty.

Just like the room.

And despite pleading with Ajax not to send her Lyle, seeing as Levisha was available, he sent him her way anyway. Stripped of her best wigs, nightgowns, perfumes and jewelry, she was now seated on the edge of the mattress wearing a pair of grey sweatpants and a ripped up shirt. Ajax had split her stylish clothing between Beverly and Levisha, forcing Shayla to wear Levisha's STD laced underwear and tattered garbs.

The monster even gave her radio away.

His reasoning was simple. He wanted the fall from grace to be atrocious and difficult and he had succeeded.

When it was time Lyle walked into the room calmly, undressed in front of her and quietly folded his pants neatly on the bed. Then he sat next to her and placed his cold hand on her thigh. "Get on your knees." His breath smelled of dried piss over sweaty gym socks.

But Shayla stood up, walked between his thighs, dropped to her knees and positioned herself between his legs. In the past he couldn't afford her and just like the other John's who realized she was on the market now, he was excited that she had been removed from glory. Normally whores were reduced a level or two after contracting some sort of illness but she could have herpes on her lips and he would care less, he wanted her badly.

"What would you like?" She asked looking up at him. She tried to smile before attempting to remove his penis from his white boxers.

"Hold up a minute, I don't wanna rush this." He extended his hand, palm in her direction. "Be easy and slow."

She frowned but immediately changed her expression to a half smile. After all, customers were always right. "Forgive me, sexy, I'm just so excited about pleasing you that I rushed you a little. My apologies."

He glared down at her. "You think you still running shit don't you? You think you in charge?" He paused. "Do you remember all those times I walked by you in this house and you passed me without so much as a smile? Without so much as a hello? Fucking red bitches! I should kill you!" He yanked her hair and pulled it backward. "Guess what, I'm in charge and I want this done my way." He released her hair.

With heavy breath she tried to remain calm but his legend preceded him and so she was fearful before he even walked into the room. Plus Ajax packed her schedule so thick that she had another customer in fifteen minutes so time was not on her side. The last thing she wanted was Ajax being angrier than he always was. In that moment she had two mad men to worry about.

"I understand, Lyle. And I wish I could sit with you all night but—"

"But what?" He yelled, spitting as he spoke. Drops of saliva slapping at her face. "You think just cause you pretty you can say and do anything you want to niggas? You think nobody gonna call you on it?"

She frowned. "You know what, it's time for you to go, Lyle. I forgot there's something I have to do anyway." She tried to stand but he yanked her wrists and pulled her down where he liked her. On her knees.

He frowned. "What do you have to do that's more important than me? And where do you think you going? NOWHERE! Because I'm not finished with you."

"I need to go get Ajax because this ain't working!"

"You know what, bitch!" He reached behind himself, grabbed a sock that looked harmless to her at first.

It wasn't.

Instead when he raised it and she saw it hung heavy in the air she realized it was filled with rocks. Unfortunately it was too late for her to flee because he brought it down on the top of her head, knocking her out immediately.

When she came to, an hour later, she was perched in the tub with cold water running all over her body from the shower. Her arms and legs were tied at the ankles and wrists but she couldn't get out of the knots. It didn't stop her from trying her hardest to set herself free. She roared and wiggled even though every part of

By T. Styles   149

her body ached. After the water dampened the knots enough she was finally able to shake free and get out of the tub, dripping wet.

Standing next to the toilet she was about to move for the door when Lyle busted inside with shiny brass knuckles. She recognized them from the past and knew they belonged to Ajax. A mouth full of white teeth he said, "I see the cold shower I gave you worked. You're up and I prefer it that way."

"Please just leave," she sobbed. "I won't tell anyone what you did here. I just want you gone."

"Now why would I do that when we just getting started?" He paused. "I paid for extra time for you and I'm gonna take every moment."

"What do you want from me?" She sobbed heavily. "Why do all of this?"

"I hate pretty bitches! I hate ho's like you!" He stomped deeper into the bathroom and hit her in the face with a closed fist, forcing her to the cool floor. Her bloody handprints smeared on the tile as her mind rolled a mile a minute.

Through all of the pain she gained clarity. She needed to be smart if she was going to survive. "Okay, okay," she said getting up, blood everywhere. "I'll do...I'll do whatever you want. Just don't hit me any more."

"I know you gonna do what I say!" He paused. "That's what I been trying to get through to you! You gonna feel it too."

She sat on the closed toilet seat. "Just tell me what you want and you won't have anymore problems from me. Whatever it is, I won't say a word."

"It doesn't matter if you say something or don't because Ajax sent me to beat you until you realize how good you had it." He paused. "So that's what I'm gonna do and then I'm gonna fuck you raw. It's gonna be my pleasure."

Shayla was laid out on the cold, pissy tile in the bathroom when Beverly entered, crossed her arms over her chest and grinned. "Well, well, well," she said slyly. "The pretty princess ain't so pretty anymore." She looked at a gold watch on her arm, which originally Shayla owned. "And let me tell you a secret, he beat you so good he worked up an appetite. Now he downstairs eating Pat's fried chicken. That mean he getting charged up just to start beating your ass all over again."

Shayla looked at her and shook her head and dropped her head back down. "Just leave me alone."

"As if you couldn't use a little company." Beverly shrugged. "After all, what else are you doing?"

"You know, when this is all said and done, that you die right?"

Beverly laughed. "See, now you hurt my feelings." She pointed down at her. "So let me go downstairs and make a few more suggestions to Lyle on how he can fuck you up even better. I'm a wealth of information you know?" She turned to walk out and came back. "Oh, and I love my new room too, so thank you for not knowing how good you had it. It smells so Purdy, just like me."

When Shayla came to, she was wrapped in bloody bandages and staring into the big-brown eyes of Bernice who was smiling and rubbing her hair on the thin mattress in her room. "Where is Lennon?" Shayla whispered, when she pulled her pasty lips apart. Her throat so dry it was difficult to speak. "Why hasn't he been by to check on me? To check on us?"

Bernice looked at the door and back at her to be sure no one was entering. "Ajax keeping us apart," she whispered. "He says the three of us were too close and he had to separate us. So we can remember who brought us together."

A tear rolled down her face. "Bernie, what we gonna do?"

"I have an idea."

Shayla sat up and gazed at her with hopeful eyes. Her body ached tremendously. "What is it?"

"You gotta stop thinking about leaving, Shayla." She played with her own fingers. "You gotta realize this is it for us and it's make believe out there. Ajax says if you stop rebelling, he'll even put you back in your pretty room. Give you some new clothes and everything." Her eyes widened. "Better than the ones Beverly wearing. You'll really be a movie star now."

Shayla squinted. "He sent you in here didn't he?"

"No! I came in here because—"

"You a trader, Bernice! Stop lying!" She paused. "What he promise you?"

"Nothing…I—"

"What the fuck did he promise you?"

Bernice's stomach bubbled and she placed her hand on her belly to calm it down. "To let me go to the beauty shop, that way I can get my hair done sometimes. I always wanted to know how it would feel. But it don't mean I'm disloyal."

"Just what I thought." Shayla shook her head. "You are no longer my sister."

Bernice eased out of bed and looked down at her. "But I—"

"Get out!" Shayla paused. "I don't fuck with you and you're dead to me!"

"Don't say that!"

"GET OUT!" Shayla turned around, grabbed a glass of water from the table next to the bed and threw it at her. It grazed the top of Bernice's hair. "Now before I beat your ass!"

Large tears huddled in the wells of her eyes. "I'll leave, Shayla. But I will always love you." She trudged toward the door, looked back once and ran out crying.

CHAPTER NINE

SHAYLA

Shayla's life took an even worse turn when she refused to clean up herself. She was a funky human. The other whores talked about her and Levisha commented that she was nastier than she'd ever been. And they were right. At the moment she sat in the middle of the floor, steeped in her own urine, hopeless.

It had been weeks since she had sex with a man willingly. As a result they would flow into her room and rape her as she lie face down, motionless like a blowup doll. Even in her immobile state, she proceeded to annoy Ajax to no end. Although he did everything in his power, including beat her repeatedly, she refused to give in and be his prize ho anymore. So after keeping Lennon away from her for weeks Ajax finally gave in.

He would send his best bet to get her to clean up her act.

Entering Shayla's room Lennon grabbed his nostrils and squeezed them tightly. Shayla took to defecating on herself, while lying face down on the bed, arms and feet out the sides. "Wow, Shayla. You smell…horribly."

She raised her head to look at him, shook it from left to right and dropped it back on the bed. Now she was staring at his size 14 red patent leather pumps instead of his face. "What you want?"

He sat on the edge of the bed and it squeaked under his weight. "Shayla, you can't keep doing this to your father." He placed his hand in the middle of her back. "If you don't work soon he *will* hurt you. He may even kill you. Is that what you want?"

She smiled. "He can't hurt someone who doesn't care." She took a deep breath and sighed. "Let him do whatever."

"Trust me…you don't mean that." He rubbed her back harder. "He just wants to make sure you are doing your part around here that's all. He's even been spending more time with Bernice and me, to show us we different from the other girls, which is what we always wanted. Took us out to dinner and everything so—"

"Why doesn't he just kill me?" Slowly her eyes met his and tears filled the well of her eye. "Why doesn't he just do what he always wanted and take my life?" She paused. "I can sense his hate for me, Dad-Ma. Why doesn't he just put a bullet in my head so I can be free? I don't have anything to live for anyway. I'm begging him too."

"You know he would never do that, Shayla." He took a deep breath. "He's never gonna let you go." He paused. "He's never gonna let any of us go. Ain't he convinced you of that if nothing else?"

She glared. "What you want?"

Lennon took a deep breath. "Why haven't you spoken to Bernice?"

"It's my business."

"Well, because you refuse to work she's been given your visitors and hers. Including that...Lyle monster." She shook his head. "She has him tonight." He placed his hand on top of his head and dropped it by his side. "Don't you see? She's tired but more importantly she's weak, Shayla."

"Too bad. All she cares about is herself." She paused. "Does she like her hair? Since that's why she betrayed me in the first place."

"That child hasn't had a relaxer ever. She don't know how to work her natural hair like you and I. What's wrong with wanting to be pampered once?"

She paused. "There's nothing more she wants than to love you. But when she comes by you ignore her. Why?"

"I have nothing else to say to you, Lennon," she said through clenched teeth. "Please leave."

Slowly Lennon rose and adjusted the boa around his neck. "You gonna fall hard behind all this bitterness, child. And it will be the most painful period you can imagine." He pointed at her. "You think you know what it feels like to be alone. You have no idea, girly, until you actually are."

He walked out and slammed the door behind himself.

DAYS LATER

Shayla's door opened when Bernice toddled inside. Shayla was under the covers, lying on her side, back faced in her direction. Although Shayla hadn't bothered to look her way Bernice knew she was up and that was all she needed to speak her mind.

"I know you're awake, Shayla, and I know you still hate me although I hate it so much. You don't have to talk. I have something to say." Tears poured down Bernice's face. "I want to apologize for ever allowing someone to come between us. Nothing means more to me than you." She paused. "And I want to thank you for...for what you did in—"

Shayla glared her way. "Don't say what you're about to say."

"I'm sorry...I..." Bernice sat on the edge of the bed and touched her leg softly.

"When I first came into that apartment we lived in, I begged God to give me a sign that my life wouldn't be so bad. That my life wouldn't stay so terrible, Shayla." She wiped the tears away with both hands. "And then you were so nice to me. You made me feel like everything was going to be okay. And then what did I do?" She took a deep breath. "Betray your trust by being Ajax's spy. He's never did anything nice for me and I hurt you badly." She paused. "And I hope you will forgive me."

Bernice stood up and walked around the bed to see Shayla's face clearly. Her eyelids were pressed together and it was obvious she was doing her best to fake sleep, just to avoid Bernice. "Is there anything I can do to show you how sorry I am, Shayla? Anything I can do, to make you forgive me?"

"No," she said under her breath.

Bernice inhaled. "I heard your bathroom got fixed. Can I use it?"

Shayla shrugged. "I don't care what you do."

"Okay, I'm going to leave you alone now. Just wanted you to know that I love you."

When she tottered into the bathroom and shut the door, Shayla opened her eyes and looked at the door before closing her eyes again. Silence filled the space and then after several minutes she heard a thump.

At first she didn't move.

But curiosity won her over and she shuddered toward the bathroom, opened the door and stumbled backward. Bernice was hanging from the shower rod, eyes open, tongue hanging out the side of her mouth.

She committed suicide.

Shayla passed out.

A WEEK LATER

Lennon opened the door and the room smelled worse than it ever had. Because Shayla had refused to eat her body had gotten so frail he could see the bones in her naked frame as she lie on the bed. This time he didn't bother to attempt to speak reason to her. Instead he lifted her tiny body up, walked her to the bathroom and placed her in the tub. Next he ran warm water over her skin and when it was filled halfway he left her there and kept the door open so he could see her clearly.

Afterward Lennon removed the soiled urine and feces covered sheets. When he was done he cut the water off in the tub and cleaned the room with bleach and Pine Sol, peeking into the bathroom every so often to make sure she hadn't drowned.

Lennon understood why she was taking Bernice's death so hard. Bernice's suicide was difficult for everyone, the whores in the house too but it was

Shayla who fell deeper into depression after ignoring her when she attempted to express love and remorse.

Although Shayla didn't utter a word since Bernice's death, Lennon could tell she was blaming herself. And he had seen enough people guilt themselves to an early grave to know that she was on her way.

When the room was cleaned he walked back into the bathroom and washed Shayla up thoroughly. She was so dirty the water was murky and her nails looked like she dipped her fingers into black paint. He had to wash her three times. When she was clean he dried her off and carried her to her bed, before placing some clean clothing on her body.

He laid her upper body in his lap, rocked her softly and chanted, "Okay...let's deal with the tough stuff now." He took a deep breath. "There's no deeper guilt than ignoring someone who came to you out of love, only for that person to die." He paused. "But that's done now. You did it and its nothing you can do to change it." He took a deeper breath. "Now you have to let the pain out, Shayla. Or it's gonna choke you."

She remained as taut as a pulled rope as he rocked her.

"Let it out, Shayla. You gotta let it go and you gotta let it go now."

Again she remained still although when he looked down at her he could see her eyes getting glassy.

"It wasn't your fault, Shayla. Do you hear me? Bernice's death wasn't your fault. Life had gotten to her long before you met her that's for sure and you got to let it go."

She wiggled a little and started whimpering. It was clear she wasn't trying to release the pain.

"Let the pain go, Shayla! Let it go! That child would not want you to be like this. She would not want you to be in so much pain, you have to let it go. Now!"

Suddenly a yowl filled with the agony of everything bad she experienced in life exited her body. She cried from her heart and she cried from her soul and all he could do was rub her back, rock her and tell her how much he cared. She cried so heavily that the clean t-shirt he just put on her was drenched with tears.

When she was done her stomach ached and she looked at him and said, "Take the pain away, Dad-Ma. Take it from my heart because if you don't when you leave I'm gonna…I'm gonna…take my life too. I can't live like this. I just can't!"

"Don't say that." He nodded. "You'll be okay, baby. You just have to —"

"But I can't! You not listening to me! I have nothing to live for!" She sat up and looked at him. "I'm begging you to make this pain go away."

He frowned. "What are you asking?"

She stared at him for what seemed like an eternity. "You know what I want. Please don't make me say it."

Lennon looked out into the room and took a deep breath. When he was ready he dug into his purse and removed his heroin kit. Raising a small bag he said, "You're right…this will make the pain go away. For a moment when you take it you'll experience a blissful feeling so controlling you'll wonder why you hadn't done this before. But, afterward, right afterward, you'll experience complete hell." He took a deep breath. "You ready for that too?"

CHAPTER TEN

SHAYLA

1994

Shayla stood on the corner with four other prostitutes, around her age as she waited for a Kerb Crawler, co word for a John or man who enjoyed having sex with prostitutes. She was as thick as fuck and her body screamed FUCK ME.

When a cool breeze came through and stroked her scalp, she fingered her crimped hair lightly, before reaching into her purse and smoothing Juniper Breeze lotion on her skin so she smelled fresh.

In the past she received her clients based on word of mouth. She barely had to leave her room but now that she had developed a habit, Ajax had lost the respect for her he had left and tossed her on the stroll. The only good part of the fall from grace was that from where they stood on the block, she could turn around and see the big yellow brothel, which she lived in.

Things had taken a wrong turn in her life that was certain.

After Bernice died Shayla took to heroin hard, using it every day. During the times she didn't have the painkiller she was haunted in her room by the image of Bernice hanging herself, moments after begging her to just talk to her. If only Shayla had given her half of her time, she would be alive.

"It's been slow out here," Kristy said with her hands on her hips, eyes on the streets. She was a frail white girl with thick red hair. "Almost eight o'clock and nothing." She looked up and down the block. "If I don't get somebody Ajax might kill me this time. Matter of fact I know he will."

"As slow as things have been he needs all girls on dick," Shayla replied. "You'll live."

"You mean on deck."

Shayla frowned. "You heard what I said."

They both giggled. "I'm serious, Shayla. I don't have a bond as close as you do with him. He's willing to dump me at anytime if I don't produce."

Shayla knew she was right although she didn't feel worthy by being a favorite. In her opinion he treated favorites worse.

Ajax found Kristy ten months back when she relocated from Pittsburgh. Her fiancé at the time brought her to Baltimore on a surprise vacation and the next morning he left her a note saying he didn't want to be with her anymore. Turned out the entire vacation was just a ruse to get her out of his home so he could be with another woman.

When she realized her life in Pittsburgh was over she had to find money and that's when Ajax swooped in. He fed her, clothed her and put her on the stroll quicker than she could understand what was happening in the Ho World.

Shayla felt empathy towards Kristy but after losing Bernice she was determined not to get too close to anyone. Besides, having emotions in this line of work could do nothing but cause problems. If she was going to survive she had to focus on self.

"Yeah, it's been slow but it'll pick up," Shayla said. "We just have to—"

Kristy grabbed her arm. Dread owned her expression. "He said if I don't bring money in tonight, I wouldn't have to work again. When I asked him what that meant he smiled and walked away." She squeezed her harder. "Shayla, I'm scared."

She released her grip and Shayla rubbed her flesh just as a white Buick pulled up to the block. Shayla,

Kristy and a few other girls stood at attention hoping to be chosen. It didn't matter what the John's wanted all the girls were ready.

This particular car stopped directly in front of Shayla.

She was about to slide inside when she glanced over at Kristy and saw her looking back at the yellow brothel, in fear for her life.

It was sad.

Shayla always got the dude and this was a common affair. If Shayla was outside they always wanted her, which was one of the reasons Ajax kept her protected in the house in the earlier days.

Shayla stepped back from the car. "You know what...go ahead," She said to Kristy.

He frowned. "But I don't want her," the John said. "I want—"

Shayla opened the door. "She's better than me. Trust me." She winked at Kristy who crawled into his car and slammed the door shut before he could change his mind.

"Yeah...whatever." He rolled his eyes, looked at her and pulled off.

The moment she entered the car another driver pulled up in a polished red Acura Legend. He was blasting *Regulate* by *Warren G featuring Nate Dogg* and the speakers pumped so loudly it caused her heartbeat to skip a few beats. When he turned down the music she noticed the inside of the luxury ride was the color of light skin. Once the driver rolled the window down, the lustful smell of CK ONE cologne teased her senses. The vehicle definitely belonged to someone with money.

Peeking further inside she focused her attentions on the driver. He looked like someone who popped out of a Thug Luscious magazine, not a man who would be cruising the streets looking for prostitutes. Basically he could get any woman he wanted.

She couldn't gauge his height but there was no denying he was extremely attractive. Dark brown with fine hair, which he kept low, his eyes were wide and the lashes that surrounded them added a soft appeal to his intense stare.

She'd fucked many men who were easy on the eyes but this man was by far the most handsome. It wasn't like she only sexed the beautiful ones. For attractiveness wasn't required to sleep with hoes but it was definitely refreshing.

She leaned down to his window and placed her hands on her knees. "What you need?"

"Get in…"

Shayla looked at the flashy car once more, opened the door and slid inside. "What…what you need?" She grinned. "I can —"

"My dick sucked." He said firmly. "Got a place or do you wanna do it in the alley?" He was stern and almost cold. "Makes no difference to me I just need it done."

She nodded and pointed to the yellow house where she lived. "I have a room there if you wanna go. It ain't the best but we can —"

"It don't matter where we go." Without another word he pulled off and drove up the block. They could've walked but it was literally across the street and up a little so leaving the car and walking would've been less discreet, despite the distance. Using her peripheral vision she checked him out but he hadn't once looked her way.

He was all business, almost to the point of being violent.

Once inside her room she walked over to the bed and sat on the edge. "You gonna stay over there or—"

"On your knees." His nostrils flared with each word. "That's how I like it."

"Okay...guess you know what you want." A little embarrassed by his forwardness, she switched over to him, dropped to her knees and undid his pants. Looking up at his face she removed his penis and placed the length of his dick into her mouth. He looked away, as if he were thinking of someone else. His warm skin smelled of soap, a welcome retreat from what she'd become accustomed to, especially since her fall from grace.

She was a magician and could feel him softening under her touch, without going fully weak. Without words she continued to engulf him until the hairs at the base of his dick tickled her lips. Her tongue sat at the bottom of his stick and she gargled a little until he was tucked neatly into her mouth and he felt her vibration. Checking to see if he was enjoying himself, she glanced up at him and suddenly he didn't seem so tough anymore.

Still, something in her spirit told her she should fear him.

Focusing on her money, she bobbed her head back and forth while gurgling her throat softly so that the tip of his dick would be trapped in a constant tremor. She had gotten into it so much that not even a full two minutes later she was rewarded with his cream down her throat.

She swallowed, stood up and wiped the corners of her mouth. "Did you like it?"

He nodded briskly, pulled two hundred dollars from his pocket for a job that cost $50 which he already paid for. "Thanks."

"You don't have to pay that much it's —"

"Do what you want with the rest, I'm out." Tossing the cash to the floor he fastened his pants and exited her room.

Surprised by his generosity she quickly picked up the money, walked to the bed and inhaled it. Even the bills smelled like him and all she could do was hope they'd meet again. And then she remembered. For what? Nobody loved a whore, not even God so there was no need in getting excited.

She separated the fifty from the other money and tucked it under her mattress just as Beverly walked into the room. Feeling herself as usual, she sauntered up to Shayla and extended her fingers. "Cash please." Shayla handed her the fifty and Beverly said, "The rest?"

This moment was major.

Because if she told her she had extra money she wouldn't be able to buy heroin on the side if need be. But if she lied and Ajax knew about the extra money, her troubles could be worse.

Taking a deep breath she trudged over to the bed lifted the mattress up and handed her the other funds. Beverly grinned and counted the money in front of her. "Next time don't be slick by tucking bills, bitch. Me and Ajax know everything that goes on around here. Remember that when you want to be sly." She rolled her eyes and slammed the door.

For some reason Beverly didn't tell Ajax that she attempted to hide money under the bed. Kristy said Beverly may have been growing a little soft but Shayla thought otherwise. Something told her she kept the extra money for herself and Shayla didn't care either which way.

Just as long as she didn't tell Ajax.

Besides, she got her first wish.

Her handsome stranger came back the next day and every week afterward for four weeks straight. Each time he visited he would be short in his demands to her. *'Get on all fours.' 'Lay flat on your back, legs up.' 'Spread your ass cheeks.'*

Not to mention she knew nothing about him because unlike the others he wasn't a conversationalist. The only thing she was certain of was that whenever he came he was angry. Someone or something wronged him in the world and for relief he fucked the hell out of her. A few times she tried to spark conversation but each time he would ignore her, leave a big tip, which she would give solely to Beverly or Ajax when he left.

His money had been so good and loyal that she started taking care of herself and as a result, Ajax gave her a nicer room and threw Levisha's funky ass back in her old digs which the girl abhorred. But everything he did was calculating. Lately a few of his regular customers stopped coming and that included Lyle and a few others. So without Shayla bringing in the big bucks he would be hurting so he needed her happy.

With the stranger coming on a regular, Shayla even smiled more and the fact that he'd been back every day gave her something to look forward to. The handsome stranger and the heroin actually made things a little easier to stomach.

After crimping her hair she was preparing to hit the streets when Ajax entered the room. The moment she saw his face, now riddled with a few wrinkles due to constant scowling, her stomach bubbled. "Hi...I'm...I'm going out now."

"Wait awhile." He walked deeper inside and closed the door. "I want to talk to you about something that's sitting on my mind."

She glanced at the clock on the wall because for the past few days her visitor came at 7:30ish which meant she had fifteen minutes at the most. If she wasn't there her fear was that he'd leave or grab Kristy or her worst case, Beverly and she'd lose him forever. "But I need to —"

"How do you like your new room?"

"It's nicer...thank you."

"Well I'm putting you back in the house full time." He stepped closer and grabbed a strand of her stiff mane. "And why do you do this to your hair?" He frowned. "You mess up the structure of your natural curls when you keep doing this."

"I'm sorry, I won't do it as much." She swallowed. "And you don't have to bring me back inside. I like it out there. It's not as bad."

He laughed and crossed his arms over his chest. "You are something else. I put you on the streets to punish you and you love it. Just Teflon."

"I don't love it, I like it." She smiled.

He frowned and struck her with the back of his hand, knocking her to the floor. Blood sat in the corner of her mouth and ran down her chin. "I don't wanna hear what you like, bitch!"

"I'm sorry."

"Dauber tried you last week and said you didn't smell the same as when he had you all them years back. And Dauber is one of my favorite customers. I need him to be happy."

"Daddy, I do all I can to stay fresh. I wash, douche and—"

"He didn't say you smelled nasty, Shayla. Just not the same." He removed a towel from his pocket and wiped the blood off his hand. "From here on out I want you in this house. If I need you back outside I'll let you know."

"Okay," she said lowering her head.

"Be grateful. You don't have the stank Kristy and Levisha have just yet. Relish in this moment because all whores rot. And I do mean all ho's."

CHAPTER ELEVEN

SHAYLA

It was midnight and Shayla stood in the open window, naked, looking into the city. A cigarette sat between her fingers and smoke clouds hovered over her head as she puffed into the air.

She already fucked her recent client Dauber and wanted him to bounce but he hung around like he was waiting on a tip. She needed his ass gone. She was waiting on Lennon to bring more dope since she was placed back on house duty or as she called it house arrest.

"Your body's perfect you know?" Dauber said as he slipped back into his jeans. "It has to be the coldest I've ever seen. Makes me wonder what's a girl like you doing here?"

She chuckled hard, throwing her head backwards so that the reverberation could escape and move upward. This nigga had her all kinds of fucked up. She took a pull from her cigarette and exhaled.

"What difference does it make how I look? What you gonna do? Get me off these streets? You gonna save my life and tell me how beautiful I am every day?" She laughed harder. "Well that young girl who needed saving died along time ago. All that's left is this old ho so save your breath. You annoying the fuck out of me."

He slipped into his shirt and grabbed his keys and wallet. "You use to be fun but now —"

"Just get the fuck out of my room." She laughed. When he didn't leave she yelled, "NOW!"

He sprinted out and slammed the door behind himself.

Five minutes later Lennon entered, his face was badly beaten as usual. Ajax had gotten to him so much Shayla believed he taunted him on purpose just to get slapped around aka some Ho Attention. "You ready for your next client, Shayla? You cleaned up right?"

Shayla smashed her cigarette out on the wall and switched over to the bed. Grabbing the edge of the sheet she squatted slightly and wiped her pussy with it. "Now I am."

He was disgusted. "What's wrong with you?" He frowned. "I'm not the one who forced you back into the house. Besides, most girls hate that job. Who would think you liked being on the stroll?"

"Well I preferred being outside because at least I felt alive." She shook her head. "But leave it to Ajax to kill my dreams as usual." She walked over to him. "You got the dope?" She looked at his hands.

He sighed. "Ajax said not until your final client. Something about you being lazy in bed the last time you were high and he got a complaint. With people not coming like they used to we have to make sure you're focused."

"Please, Lennon, I...I don't think I can wait that long." She begged. "Plus nobody else is waiting on me. Who cares if I get a little —"

"Yes he is. He's downstairs. Been here the entire time, was waiting on Dauber to leave that's all."

Shayla walked to the bed and flopped on it. "But I don't think I can make it without my medicine."

"I know...just finish with him and I promise I'll get you something later. Okay?"

Shayla nodded, having no choice anyway. "Okay...okay." Her head hung low. "Whatever."

Lennon placed a firm hand on her shoulder and squeezed. "I'll go get him." She walked out.

Alone in her room, Shayla stared at the floor and thought of Bernice again. She missed her terribly. She wondered if she was happy in the ever after and if she was looking down at her. Maybe even protecting her sometimes. Although guilt still sat in Shayla's heart over the suicide, she wondered if she wasn't better off being dead. She even thought about hanging herself except she didn't have a shower rod in her new room.

Soft knocks rattled the door.

She grabbed her pink silk robe, walked to the door and opened it. She was now looking at the handsome stranger who saw her almost every day. At first she smiled until she realized he was all about the business like the others. So she flopped down on the mattress because there was nothing to be excited about.

"What you want today?" Her head hung.

"What's wrong with you?" This was new. Never had he asked what she felt.

"What do you want today?" She repeated, not up for talking anymore.

He walked in and closed the door. Sitting in a chair across from the bed he folded his arms over his chest. "I asked a question."

"Well you not paying me to answer questions."

"Correction. I'm paying you to do whatever the fuck I say. And right now I asked a question I want answered."

She looked at him and sighed. "I don't know. Guess I don't feel well."

He shook his head. "Guess you just another dope fiend too. I'm not surprised though. If you in the streets you can't be good for nobody."

"Are you here for something or not?" She paused. "By something I mean sex."

"Nah...right now I'm gonna just stare at you." He said sarcastically.

"So you gonna waste your money being ridiculous?" She paused. "Like I believe that."

"Try me." And that's what he did. For the entire hour he sat across from her on the bed and watched as she shivered and went through withdrawal. When his time was up he rose, looked at his watch and walked out.

Shayla was a wreck when later that day Lennon returned with her medicine. Luckily for her he doped her up and put her to bed. Surprisingly when Shayla woke up he was still on the mattress, behind her. He stroked her arm and she sat up straight and yawned. "I thought you'd be gone by now."

"I wanted to watch you sleep."

She frowned. "Something feels off. What's wrong?"

"You hate me now don't you?" Lennon asked.

"Why you say that?"

He sighed. "Did you know I always wanted a daughter? That I always wanted you?"

She rubbed her arms. "For what? So she can be a ho?"

"No...and I realize it might seem that way but no, that's not it." He exhaled and sat up. "I knew if I could just be a mother to someone I could always receive that love in return." He touched her face with his rough hands. "I just didn't know how strong you had to be as a parent. I didn't know you had to put yourself second to your child and even your man because if not...then someone else could...could turn your child into this." He looked at her.

Shayla sighed. "Where is my real mother?"

"I don't know, Shayla." Tears welled in his eyes as he continued to stare at her. "I really don't. I swear it's true."

She flopped back down, closed her eyes and reopened them. Her expression was pained. "I don't know who I am, Lennon." She placed her hand on her chest. "I don't know who I'm supposed to be and I'm angry because of it. I'm feeling like…like if I don't find a release soon I'll have to do what I can to get by." She took a deep breath. "Do you know what I mean?"

Lennon sat up and placed his hand on her thigh. He wiped the tears from his own face and used his thick, hard, flat thumb to wipe hers away roughly, smearing her eye makeup. "There I go getting you all confused in the make believe world again. We ho's, Shayla and this is it for us. Beds, dope and money." He took a deep breath. "Now go clean yourself up. I left a little something on the table for later."

Ajax put her outside for the day and Shayla had been on the block for hours when suddenly she was hungry. With the five dollars she was allowed for a meal, she walked to a diner down the block and sat at a table.

Immediately a waitress saw her waiting and from where she stood she could also see Shayla wasn't wearing panties under her purples skirt. Irritated, she strolled up to her, removed the pencil and pad from her pocket and licked the tip of the pencil before asking, "What you having?"

Nervously, Shayla opened and closed her legs while looking through the menu. She was trying to find out what she could afford. "Just eggs and toast please."

"What you drinking?"

"Water. Thank you," she smiled.

The waitress walked away but turned back toward the table. "You know what, sweetie, you should really close your legs. This here is a family business and kids don't need to be seeing your snatch."

Shayla looked up at her and cleared her throat. "Sorry." The waitress rolled her eyes and walked away, as Shayla slammed her legs together tightly.

She was waiting on her meal when the handsome John walked up to Shayla's table. The moment he sat down she could smell his cologne and for some reason under the lights of the diner she felt insecure. In her room she was in control but now…"You not working?" He asked. "'Cause I was looking for you."

"I'm working later…just…just getting something to eat." She adjusted her spaghetti strap shirt and fingered her hair nervously hoping he didn't see her under the harsh lights of the strobe and got turned off.

"What you eating?" He grabbed the menu and glanced down at it on the table. "They steak good?"

She shrugged. "I don't know. I never had it. Can only afford the eggs."

He looked up at her. "You fuck 24/7 and you can't even afford a steak?"

Hurt, she was about to leave when he said, "Sit down."

For some reason she obeyed just as the waitress walked over with her usual funky attitude. And then the waitress saw his face. Suddenly her hair got a little attention as she plucked the dead curls outlining her face and even straightened her uniform. Removing the pencil and pad seductively she said, "Hey…can I help you, handsome?"

"Yeah, let me get two orders of steak, eggs and cheese. Bring out two fruit punches too."

She looked at Shayla and back at him. "She already ordered eggs."

"How 'bout you eat that and bring what the fuck I asked for," he said firmly.

"Uh…yes…of course." The waitress jotted his order down and left in a hurry, as she was embarrassed as fuck.

"Thank you." Shayla said in a low voice. "For the steak."

He shrugged. "Can't have you hungry when we do what we do in your room."

She nodded. "So what you want?" She paused and looked down at the table. "When we go back to…you know…the house?"

"Let me feed you first." He looked around the diner at everyone but her. "We'll get into all that other shit later."

She nodded. "Well can I at least have your name?"

He chuckled once. "I can do that. It's Gunner."

She smiled. "Like a weapon?"

"Just like it."

The meals came fifteen minutes later and he dove into his steak like he hadn't eaten all day or was just released from prison. He was halfway finished his meal when he noticed she hadn't taken a bite. "I never asked you this before but what's your name?" He asked.

"Shayla."

He nodded. "Well, Shayla, eat up. If a nigga buy you a meal it's rude to waste it. And I don't waste shit."

CHAPTER TWELVE

SHAYLA

Shayla was straightening her sheets and fluffing her pillows as the sun spilled into the room. In a good mood, afterward she brushed her natural curly hair and placed it into a bun when Ajax walked inside. When she spotted him the brush dropped from her clasp. "Something wrong?" She asked.

He smiled. "Why are you afraid of me?"

"I...don't think I am...not anymore."

He frowned and walked deeper inside. "Well you shouldn't be afraid because I would never hurt you deliberately." He paused. "Every strike I've dealt you, every blow to the face was to make you stronger. You believe that don't you?"

She nodded. "Of course."

He rubbed her mane. "I like it better when your hair is like this. Natural and soft." He released it. "Go put on that red pants suit that Dauber bought you eight months back. I'm taking you to your first nice restaurant."

She didn't trust him and preferred not to be alone with him. But what could she do but relent? "S...sure, daddy. Give me five minutes."

He marched out and closed the door. Now alone she placed her palms on her dresser and breathed heavily as she stared at her reflection in the mirror. "What do you want now?"

The dark décor was romantic in La 'Quoi Steakhouse in Washington DC which gave Shayla pause. She and Ajax were seated at a round table, candles lit in front of them, two large glasses filled with red wine at their reach. It looked like they were on a date. Except she was as stiff as stone.

"Drink, Shayla, this is your night." He grabbed his glass and raised it in the air before taking a sip and placing it back down.

She glanced around the ritzy place and her hand shivered as she picked up her glass, spilling a little wine on the white tablecloth by accident in the process.

Embarrassed, he rose up, preparing to strike her with the back of his hand when she said, "Please don't!" She paused. "I'm sorry."

Slowly he reclaimed his seat and his emotions after seeing people watching. "It's okay...drink what you have left and don't make a mess."

She gulped all of her wine, sat the glass down carefully and looked at him.

He cleared his throat. "So, are you happy I brought you back into the house?"

She nodded yes.

"Then why do you do what you do?"

"I don't know what you mean."

"You know what I mean. You sabotaging me and have been for some time now. Haven't you?"

She shook her head from left to right. "I don't know what you're talking about, daddy." She shook her head briskly. "I promise."

Silence.

"And I see you have a new regular customer." He raised his wine glass and took a sip. "How is that going? He treating you okay?"

She suppressed the urge to frown knowing full well that the only thing he cared about was that hot space between her legs. Not how the men make her feel.

But the real reason for the dinner had revealed itself.

He wanted Gunner gone.

"We don't have a relationship. He comes over, pays you and leaves. Just like the others."

"Nah, you and I know he's not like the others." He drank all his wine and flagged the waiter over again. "Bring two glasses of vodka, these aren't strong enough." The waiter nodded and walked away. "He looks like someone you might be attracted to. I'm talking about the John. Someone you might want to date."

"I haven't dated anyone. Ever. Do you not want me to see him anymore?" Her heart thumped wildly as she waited for the answer. Gunner was all she had to look forward to in a life of darkness; despite knowing he never gave her the slightest inclination that he was interested in anything more than sex.

"You can see him but I want you to stop sabotaging my business and I want you to stop doing it now. You and I both know what I mean."

"Sure, daddy. Whatever you mean."

Since Shayla hadn't received any clients in the brothel she decided to go on the stroll to earn some money. Things were looking really bleak when Kristy ran up to her in a rush. She grabbed both her hands and said, "Have you heard about the Prostitute Murders?"

Shayla's eyes widened. "What?" She snatched away from her. "What you talking about now? You always coming my way with some madness."

"Girl, people been showing up murdered and there's a detective who's—"

"I prefer to introduce myself if you don't mind." When Shayla turned around an older black woman about 5'4" was looking up at her. She extended her hand and Shayla reluctantly shook it. "The name's Detective Johnson but my friends call me police." She giggled heavily.

"Detective is your first name?" Shayla asked.

"Yep…changed it when I was eighteen."

Shayla's jaw dropped. "Really?"

"I'm just joking," the detective laughed boisterously at her own witticism. "I been waiting for someone to ask me if my name was Detective for years, just so I could tell that joke." She paused. "You the first so that makes you unique."

"Uh...thank you. I think."

Det. Johnson looked over her shoulder at Kristy. "You can go now unless you have anything else to say about the case."

"No...I'm gone." Kristy took off running before she could change her mind.

She laughed. "She sure can get up can't she?" She paused. "Anyway I've driven by here before and most of the time I see your friend and the other times you. What ya'll doing out here with things going so crazy in Baltimore these days?"

Shayla's heart thumped. The last thing she wanted was to get locked up for selling pussy. She heard many crazy stories of altercations about ho's in prison. From the police officers raping them to taking their money, she wanted zero parts of the matter.

"I don't know...I was just walking home."

"Oh, you live 'round here?" The detective glanced around briefly.

Shayla glanced over at the yellow house and knew going there was out the question. "Uh...not really I—" Shayla looked at her naked arm as if she had a watch. "But my friend should be coming in a moment so I really must go."

The detective looked her over. "Listen, you seem like an ice girl but people are being murdered and I'm here to see to it that this stops. Just because men and women participate in ungodly acts doesn't mean they deserve to die in the manner that they are." She paused. "Don't you agree?"

Shayla nodded.

"Good, so for now keep your eyes peeled for any suspicious characters and I'm sure I'll be seeing you again." She looked at Shayla's small mini dress. "And for goodness sake wear something more acceptable. You're a young lady not a ho." She walked to the end of the block and jumped in her squad car before pulling off.

Shayla ran all the way home.

Gunner looked as if the world was on his shoulders when he walked into Shayla's room where she stood in the middle of the floor waiting for him. He closed the door behind himself and looked her over. Shayla knew immediately he was angry about something.

This meant rough sex.

"What you want tonight?" She asked softly.

"I don't know yet."

She nodded. "You wanna talk again?"

"Nah, this time I wanna fuck."

She bobbed her head, walked toward her bed, raised her pink chiffon dress and placed her palms on the mattress, ass in the air. "Like this?"

He shook his head no.

She stood up and the dress flowed downward. "Then what you want?"

"Role play." He paused. "You ever act? Probably not since you been in here all your life but—"

"I did some acting in the past!" Shayla's eyes lit up when she heard his request. Immediately the memories of her childhood with Lennon came to mind when they would pretend they were actresses. Way before Ajax pulled her out of her dreams and tossed her into the sex industry. "That's a good idea! I can do it." A proud expression covered her face. "You don't know but I used to be an actress as a child."

He smiled but removed it quickly. It was the first emotion she'd seen from him...ever. "Well pretend you're a dirty slut who just cheated on her husband and I'm about to throw you out of our house. Can you do that?"

She frowned because that didn't seem like what she had in mind or much fun but it was whatever. "A little serious don't you think?" She paused. "I ain't never been nobody's wife so —"

"But you been a ho though. So improvise."

She scratched her scalp, dropped her hand and looked at the floor. As hard as she tried she couldn't think of a good way to introduce the cheating wife routine. She couldn't even find a good movie to refer to in her mind. She took a deep breath and said, "I know you don't believe me but I'm sorry I hurt you. Sorry for the lies and going behind your back. You didn't deserve any of it."

"Why should I forgive you? You ain't nothing but a filthy whore."

She took another deep breath and thought about how angry he was getting. Something told her if she said the wrong thing it could mean her health. Carefully she approached. "You should forgive me because we made a vow for better or worse...and me cheating on you is the bad part but I promise the good part is coming."

His jaw twitched. "I should kill you. How about that?"

She swallowed the lump in her throat. "Please don't." She paused. "In fact...get on the bed and remove your pants. Because I think I can make it all go away."

Unrushed, he complied and when he was done he lay on the top of her mattress. He was already semi-hard and she couldn't help but notice that he was turned on. Not knowing what to do next, she walked up to him and smacked him on the left cheek. Immediately regretful she said, "I went too far. Please forgive —"

He yanked her toward him and positioned her pussy on top of his dick. "Do it again."

"Do what?"

"Hit me."

She slapped him on the right cheek.

"Again!" He demanded as he pounded into her.

She whacked him in the chest.

"Again!" He insisted as he pushed in and out of her body.

Releasing energy, she slapped his arms, face and chest. She didn't stop until she was lying on top of him, breathing into his chest from exhaustion. His body was bruised with red whelps. He busted off in her pussy a long time ago.

Slowly she rolled off of him and he scooted off the bed. Looking down at her he said, "You not gonna be here long."

She sat up and pulled the white sheet to cover her breasts. "I...I don't know what that means."

He slipped into his boxers and then jeans. "Me either...but I'll see you later."

When he walked out the door Ajax was standing in the hallway looking at her on the bed. His eyes sent chills down her spine and she wondered how much he overheard about what Gunner just said. She relaxed when she realized if he heard anything traumatic she would be dead by now.

So she lied on her side, closed her eyes and drifted to sleep, with him watching.

CHAPTER THIRTEEN

LENNON

I nside an available room in the whorehouse, Lennon stood on his knees with Johnson's dick in his ass and Samuel's thickness in his mouth. Samuel was about to come but Johnson couldn't get his rocks off because Lennon's asshole had been ripped so much from overuse, his penis kept dropping out. Frustrated Johnson removed his dick from inside Lennon and said, "This not gonna work for me, man. He too wide."

Lennon removed his mouth from Samuel and looked back at Johnson. "Let me take care of him first and I'll do you after — "

"Nah, I'll find somebody else." He pulled up his pants, fastened them and removed his portion of the money from the dresser. "Thanks anyway." He stormed out and slammed the door.

"Wait!" Lennon yelled before Samuel took his head and placed it back around his penis.

"I'm almost there, come on, fuck that nigga." It didn't take long for Lennon to pleasure him with his oral sex game so within five minutes the John was satisfied and out of his room. Lennon took the moment to brush his teeth as Ajax walked inside.

"So, you still mad at me about that gig?" Ajax asked.

"What do you think, Ajax?" He spit the toothpaste into the sink and rinsed his mouth. "You made me have sex again when you promised I'd never have to anymore."

"You've had to work in the past, Lennon. What's the real reason you mad at me?"

"Okay…" Lennon walked to his bed and flopped down. "Beverly told the girls you took Shayla out to dinner. Heard it was a nice fancy place too. You ain't never treated me like that." He sighed. "And do you know what I ate that night? Nothing because you forgot to have Levisha go for food and she had the money instead of me." He shook his head. "Is that fair to you?"

He laughed softly. "I'm gonna be honest. Things have been a little crazy for us." He sat next to him. "It's just that I need all hands on deck right now. Including yours. With our customers dwindling…what else can I do?"

Lennon nodded. He was talking foolishness but Lennon was grateful to receive any attention since lately all Ajax thought about was the girls and his money. "I'm here for you, Ajax. You know that."

"I know you are." He paused. "So have you noticed Shayla been getting the same client for weeks in a row? And ain't nothing happened to him?"

Lennon wiped his mouth with a hand towel. "No...but you want me to stop her?"

"I don't think that will be enough. So the next time he comes by I want you to follow him. Find out where he lives and I'll take it from there."

"Okay, but what about us?" Lennon paused. "Can we get back to what we used to do? Before Shayla?" He paused. "Before everybody?"

He smiled and touched the side of his face. "Do this for me and everything will be back in order." He paused. "But I need you to find out where that boy lives first. It's very important."

CHAPTER FOURTEEN
SHAYLA

Shayla walked up and down the street looking for Kerb Crawlers and police officers. Every now and again if she'd see a cop car she would act as if she were about to walk into one of the houses on the row, even if it meant going into someone else's yard.

Normally she'd be worried about running into Ajax since he wanted most of her time spent in the brothel, but she learned by working the streets in between she could tuck a little money without Ajax knowing to support her habit.

Luckily the last couple of days he hadn't been at the Brothel and as a result he put Beverly and Lennon in charge. Since both of them had clients that meant they stayed out her way and she had a little freedom.

Kristy and the other whores believed Ajax had a girlfriend on the side but Shayla would cut the rumor down, saying he was gay and loved Lennon. At least that was what Lennon made her believe while growing up.

Strolling up and down the block, as the night went on she realized it was best to go in the house in case a client dropped by when Lennon pulled up in one of Ajax's old black Cadillac's. "Get in, Shayla. We have to talk."

Her eyes widened and her breath quickened. "I wasn't doing nothing. I was just about to go to the house and—"

"I'm not Ajax. I can see in your eyes you're terrified and there's no need to be scared of me. Ever. Plus I have something for you. Something that will make you feel better."

Hearing this she pulled the door open and slid inside. When the door closed she cut her finger on a piece of shredded silver on the seatbelt and winced. "Ouch."

Lennon observed the slash. "I don't know if Ajax has any napkins but you can—"

Shayla quickly opened his glove compartment. "He does in here."

Lennon frowned but focused on the road. She was way too familiar with his car.

After cleaning up the blood she closed the compartment and asked, "You said you have something for me. Where is it?"

Lennon shook his head and pulled off. "When you gonna get clean, Shayla? The dope life doesn't become you at all. You're too far into it now."

"Maybe I'll get clean when you do."

Lennon frowned and looked at her before focusing back on the road. "You may not like your life and you may even blame me but don't forget I raised you. Show some respect."

She swallowed. "Sorry."

"I heard Ajax took you out a couple of weeks back. Did you enjoy yourself?" He chuckled. "Because I can't remember the last time he took me anywhere. I told him myself in case you think I'm barking up the wrong tree. Just wanted to get your take on it."

"Is that why you ain't been talking to me lately? Because of Ajax?"

"You know that's not it, Shayla. I gotta make money too you know?" He shrugged. "It's just been busy that's all so I haven't gotten around to spending much time with you. Besides, you know how things are in the house."

Shayla nodded. "Okay."

"So I hear you got a boyfriend," he continued. "The girls saying he's a cutie too. Now that I think about it I remember seeing him a few times myself."

Shayla nervously scratched her scalp. "I ain't got no boyfriend. Why you say that?"

"I seen the boy, Shayla. I know he ain't been around for nobody else too. And with John's not coming around like they used to and the regulars dropping off like flies good clientele is hard to come by." He paused. "So tell me, why he still around despite the drought?"

"I don't know but he's nice and he pays." Shayla shrugged. "I think that's fair don't you?"

Lennon pulled over, parked and took a deep breath. "I need to know if something more is going on with that boy. Ajax believes he —"

"You hate me," Shayla said through clenched teeth. "I can see in your eyes that you hate me. I don't know why I missed it before but it's so clear now."

"What are you talking about?" Lennon frowned. "Why would you say something like that when you know it's not true?"

"Before Ajax had me whoring, he only had you and two other girls. Then when I got old enough to lie across the bed he put me on duty too. Then money started coming in that ya'll never had before and you felt like he forgot about you. You felt like you didn't matter because as much as you hate to admit it you loved making money for him. Now you feel useless." She paused. "At the end of the day you despise me."

Lennon frowned. "And how do you figure that?"

"You told me yourself."

"What are you talking about now?" His chest puffed up. "When?"

"The day you first shot heroin in my arm."

Lennon looked around and took a deep breath. "I...I don't remember that. I don't know if you know but that day was the hardest day of my life. Bernice had killed herself and you were a wreck."

"Well you said it," she paused. "You thought I wasn't listening but I heard you say you hated me. Hated having to love me." Tears rolled down Shayla's cheeks. "You say you wanted to be a mother but not if it meant giving up Ajax. Tell the truth! You blamed me for losing him. You blame me now." She wiped the tears away. "So after awhile, I started hating you too I guess."

"Shayla...please stop."

"Why wasn't I enough for you? Why did you need him around more than me? We could've taken care of each other and I wouldn't have to be this. You wouldn't have to do that."

Lennon looked around the car and outside of it. He clutched the steering wheel and moved uneasily in his seat. She was laying it on thick and he wanted out of the situation. "Ajax says to watch you with the boy. That's what I came to tell you."

"I gotta have him, Lennon. And I know he can't love me back because nobody's capable of loving a whore but if you take him from me ...I'll—"

"Don't say it." He placed a hand on her shoulder. "I just wanted you to know what he said but it doesn't mean I support what he wants." Reaching over he grabbed her hand. "Just be careful. There's a side to Ajax you don't know about."

"There's a side to all of us that's hidden." Shayla paused. "Now do you got something for me or not? I'm not feeling too well."

CHAPTER FIFTEEN

SHAYLA

Hands on the glass, Shayla stared through the window at a boutique. A beautiful turquoise and black dress hung on a mannequin which resembled her shape. From where she stood there was a yellow tag dangling on it with a price of $19.99 and she grinned widely. Confident that for once she would be able to purchase something not pre-owned, she walked into the store proudly.

The moment the door chimed immediately the store clerk approached. The woman smiled until she moved closer and saw the tiny leather dress she wore which barely covered her legs along with the red mid drift top that almost exposed her breasts.

Her style screamed *I'M A HO.*

"What do you want?" The woman placed her hands on her hips. "Ain't no men here so if that's what you looking for get out."

Shayla smiled and tugged at her dress to pull it down in an effort to look more presentable. "But I have money right here." She removed a twenty-dollar bill from her pocket and proudly extended it to the clerk. "Um...for that dress over there." She pointed at it.

The woman looked at the damp bill and crossed her arms over her chest. "No thank you." The cashier clumped toward the door, yanked it open and placed her foot in front of it to prevent it from closing. A cool breeze crawled inside. Crossing her arms over her chest again she said, "Now take your nasty pussy ass up out of here before I call the police."

"But I have the money." She pleaded and walked up to her, extending her hand.

"Leave! Now! Your ho money is no good here."

Shayla looked at the floor, back at the dress and trudged out.

Shayla and Kristy were in Kristy's room drinking vodka and Shayla was the drunkest she'd ever been. Her feelings were hurt after being humiliated and she needed a break from it all.

Kristy provided it.

They were sitting on the bed as Kristy gave her the activities at the ho-house. "So first off Beverly got mad because Ajax made her go outside 'cause the customers not coming like they use to."

"Good! She needs to be knocked down a space or two."

"She goes outside and the first man who pulls up she starts talking shit to. I'm standing there like is she crazy or something? We supposed to be making money not making people mad." She paused. "Anyway he gets out the car, grabs her in the back of the neck and smashes her forehead through his car window." Kristy stood up and reenacted her head going through the glass. "But I think he was surprised he hit it that hard because he pushed her out the way and was mad after looking at his car."

"Oh my God!"

"Girl, guess what that bitch does?"

"What?" Shayla asked with wide eyes.

"She takes off her shoe, the red ones with the silver spikes she keeps gluing on cause they keep dropping off...and slams him in the eye with her heel." Kristy laughed. "There was so much blood coming from his face that the cops didn't care about her bashed head.

By T. Styles   213

They just locked her ass up and stitched her up in the pen."

Shayla covered her mouth. "Oh no, Ajax is gonna kill her."

"You telling me. He was 'round here all morning yelling about her and was thinking about leaving her ass in jail when he found out what happened. Especially with the cops circling because of the Prostitution Murders."

Shayla shook her head and folded her hands in her lap. "Yeah…the cop who came at me the other day, been around again. I guess she think if she keeps asking me I'll know something different."

"Yeah, and it don't help that a lot of our girls are leaving." She paused. "And what I don't get is why Ajax allowing them to go?" She glanced at Shayla.

"Why you looking at me?"

"Cause it don't add up. First he was saying none of his girls are leaving and now…"

"I can't tell you what he be thinking half the time." Shayla paused. "But what happened to the other girls?"

"Courtney called me the other day from Vegas telling me everybody going there." She paused. "Even tried to get me to come but I don't know yet."

The door opened and Levisha, entered Kristy's room. "Hey, I—"

"Ahn, uhn, bitch!" Kristy yelled rushing up to her, snatching the door from her hand and shoving her back a step. "You don't come in here without knocking. Ever! I could've had a client or something."

"My bad," Levisha said scratching her pale patchy skin. Her flesh was so horrid that although she was white nobody knew her nationality because her face was always flaming red. That didn't stop her from knowing how to suck a mean dick, bumps and all. "I'm here for Shayla. Her customer waiting."

Shayla jumped up and moved toward the door. "Who?"

Levisha grinned. "You know which one. I'm not gonna lie, I tried to keep him for myself but he wasn't having it." She shook her head. "Girl you sure are lucky. That dude be in here like he trying to take you away." She moved closer and got sad. "And if you get a chance go, Shayla. Take a chance. Weird things are happening around here. Save yourself."

By T. Styles   215

The window was open in Shayla's room and brought with it a cool breeze. They had just finished having sex and were lying on their sides faced each other. "Where you come from?" She asked. "And where do you go when you leave?"

"You smell like liquor." He yawned and rolled over on his back. "It stinks."

She grimaced. "So you not gonna answer the question?"

"Now I'm paying you to ask me questions?" He paused. "The last I remembered I make the decisions and you fulfill my requests." He smiled and her stomach fluttered. "Not the other way around."

"Who are you, Gunner?" She asked seriously. "And why do you come week after week for me?"

"I ain't up for talking about my life, Shayla."

She smiled. "Wow...you said my name real nice. I like it."

"Shayla..." He said softly. "Since you in the talking mood, tell me about you."

She giggled. "Well...let me see...my mother's a famous geisha and my daddy is a lieutenant in the military. They had me in secret and brought me to America to be a star. And then—"

"Your life that fucked up where you gotta lie about your past?" He paused. "A geisha? Really?"

She looked away. "It ain't a lie if it makes you feel better."

"True." He sat on the edge of the bed, looked out into the room and sighed. It was dark, grim and lifeless. "I can't believe I be up in here. Look at this dump. I don't belong in this place."

She sat up and looked at him with wild eyes. "So...so you not coming back?"

"That's not what I'm saying." He stood up and got dressed. "When I come back I'm gonna be ready to talk to you about some things." He walked toward a small black plastic bag. "When I do I want you wearing this." He removed the dress she wanted in the store and tossed it at her. "Later." He walked out.

At first she didn't know what she was seeing but when she saw the material of the outfit she picked it up, brought it to her nose and inhaled before breaking down crying.

He had followed her, seen her observing the dress, walked in and bought it. It was the most thoughtful thing anybody had ever done for her.

GUNNER

Gunner walked into the hallway after leaving Shayla's room and Ajax approached him. "You drink?" Ajax asked.

Silence.

Ajax chuckled. "You got words for Shayla but none for the man who made her available to you?" He paused. "You young but you can do better than that right?"

Gunner crossed his arms over his chest and observed him closely. "What's this about?"

"One drink and I'll tell you everything you need to know."

Fifteen minutes later they were downstairs in the basement of the house. A wall full of various liquors and flavors stood behind a raggedy wooden bar. Ajax bopped behind it grabbed two glasses and rinsed them out. "What you like?"

Gunner pulled out one of the barstools and plopped in it. "Vodka."

Ajax poured him a heaping glass and slid it over to him. "You know...before this place I owned a pet shop. Sold the finest Pitbulls in all colors." He poured himself a glass of whiskey before walking to the front of the bar and sitting in front of Gunner. "But there was one dog I never sold." He sipped his whiskey and sat the glass down, clasping his hands in front of him. "Not because he was no good, it was the opposite, because every dog lover wanted him.

Gunner chuckled once. "What made this dog so special?"

"Aw, man, he was beautiful." Ajax slapped the bar. "An orange pit with red eyes that I trained real good. Real tough and smart. At two the dog could do everything but cook."

"What happened to him?"

Ajax exhaled. "Was on vacation for a week and let my friend watch him. The other dogs I left in the store with my cashier but my orange pit needed special attention." He sighed. "But when I came back the dog was different. He pissed and shit everywhere and you know what I did?"

Silence.

"I killed him the next day. Cut his throat wide open to the bone." He demonstrated by running two fingers across his neck. "What you think about that?"

Gunner nodded. "I think if you wanted the dog you should've never had him on display in the first place. There's always a nigga out there who wants what you got. Remember that." He pushed the drink back toward Ajax. "It ain't no different with animals."

Ajax nodded and looked at the filled glass. "Thought you liked vodka."

"I do. But I stopped drinking that shit years ago. Haven't touched the stuff since." He slapped the counter. "Thanks though." He walked away.

CHAPTER SIXTEEN

LENNON

The dark night sky concealed Lennon who was parked a few feet back from Gunner's car. He was waiting patiently for him to come out after the diversion tactic he knew Ajax planned. When Gunner finally came out he seemed calm, and not as uncomfortable as most people did after meeting with Ajax and his sinister ways.

As if he had no cares in the world, Gunner eased in the car and pulled out of the parking lot with Lennon shadowing. He drove for fifteen miles before stopping at a small shopping center. Once there he bopped into a fried chicken carryout, stayed about twenty minutes and returned to his car with a brown paper bag. He was about to pull off when a woman approached the driver's side, reached in and hugged him.

Lennon was quick as he snapped a few pictures of the exchange on a Polaroid camera. After five minutes the girl left and Lennon took one more picture before quickly following Gunner's lead as he drove.

After twenty minutes down the road Gunner stopped at a cemetery in Landover Maryland. He grabbed the paper bag and a green and white lawn chair from the trunk and walked through the graveyard. Within a minute he disappeared into the thick brush.

"What are you doing?" Lennon said to himself. "It's dark out here."

Needing to see closer Lennon eased out, crept through the woods until he found him. Branches crackled under his high-heeled step. Careful to keep his distance, after a little detective work he saw Gunner sitting on a grave, eating a sandwich and talking to a headstone. A gun sat on the top of it. Lennon snapped one picture, unable to get more due to the sound. Afraid of getting caught or shot, he hustled back to the car and waited.

Once in his vehicle he lingered nervously as Lennon returned to his ride, driving about ten minutes to a small neighborhood. Once out the car he greeted a man in a tiny brick house who was sitting on the step drinking a beer. He and the man seemed to have a good rapport because Gunner laughed heavily with the man in front of the house. It was the first time Lennon had seem him exhibit any emotion because he handled affairs at the brothel like he was going through a car wash.

An hour later Gunner returned to his car and pulled up to a much more suburban neighborhood. The houses had lots of land between them and it was evident the owners had money. From where Lennon was parked he saw Gunner pick up a large portable cell phone in his car. And although he couldn't hear what was being said but could tell by the way Gunner's hands moved and head rocked from behind that the conversation wasn't friendly.

Five minutes later a young girl came out with an older woman holding her hand. The girl was eight-years old and she seemed tensed, like she didn't want to be there. The older woman approached Gunner when he got out and kissed him on the cheek. The younger girl crossed her arms over her chest tightly. She was not impressed with his presence in the least.

Gunner said something to the older woman and she looked at the little girl and Gunner before walking into the house. Now, Gunner was alone with the girl. He reached in his pocket and handed her a wad of money. She stuffed it in her pocket but crossed her arms again. A few minutes later the older woman

By T. Styles   223

returned and she and the younger girl walked into the house.

"Who are you, Gunner?" Lennon said to himself. "And what do you want with Shayla?"

CHAPTER SEVENTEEN
SHAYLA

Shayla stepped out of the steamy shower and wrapped a towel around her body. Since her reflection was foggy she swiped her hand over the mirror and looked at herself. Her body ached from heroin pains and she figured she had more than an hour before she'd be in severe agony. But she would have to push her discomfort to the back burner before she got high.

A knock at the door indicated that it was time to work so she took a deep breath, slipped into her pink silk nightie and walked out the bathroom to open the door.

It was Gunner.

He looked her over. "Why you not wearing the dress I bought?

"Didn't know you were coming." Her motions were jittery as she rubbed her arms.

He walked inside, leaned against the wall and tucked his hands into his pockets. She locked the door. "Your pimp don't want me around. What I can't figure out is why? I'm a paying customer. And he sells pussy. I fail to see the problem."

She looked down. "I don't know. He...he raised me. Guess he's a little over-protective."

Gunner frowned. "Raised you?"

"Yes, since I was a little girl. Maybe he doesn't like seeing me with you." She paused. "Does he have a reason to worry?"

He smiled.

She grinned. "Wow...that's a first. You always so serious. Didn't know you had another emotion."

"Put that dress on I bought." He said seriously.

"Why?"

"So I can take it off."

She walked to the dresser, dropped the nightie she was wearing to her ankles and pulled the dress out of her drawer before slipping it on. "Is this better?"

"Get into bed," he directed.

She obeyed.

Easily he pulled himself off the wall and walked toward her at the side of the bed. Kneeling on the mattress she removed his belt and pushed his boxers and jeans down. Naked from the waist down she placed her face in his crotch and inhaled. "You always smell so…so good." She touched his dick and ran her tongue around the opening before sucking him softly at first. "And your taste….mmm….so…"

He stiffened quickly and he pushed her back onto the bed. Crawling over top of her he pulled the dress over her head and looked at her smooth naked yellow body. "Fuck am I doing here?" He said to himself. "With you?"

"Whatever you want. Isn't that why you're alive?" She paused. "To do what you want?"

She smiled and he spread her legs apart entering her pussy slowly at first, before speeding up." His motions were swifter as he looked down at her face. She was perfect in a dark way.

She ran her fingers up his back. "Mmmmmmm, you feel like you…like it inside of me."

"I do," he said biting his bottom lip. "Fuck." He flipped her over and entered her pussy from behind. When her face turned to the side he pounded harder until he released himself inside of her. When he was done he rolled her over so that their eyes met.

The stare was long and intense.

Suddenly he eased out of bed, got dressed, walked to the door and stood next to it. Confused, she placed the dress back on and moved toward him. "Everything okay?"

"I wasn't prepared for you."

His eyebrows rose. "What does that mean?"

"I don't know. Guess I'm just talking." He walked out.

Lennon stood behind Shayla as she sat in a chair looking at herself in the mirror. He picked up her brown brush and swept her long hair backward. Staring down at her Lennon said, "It's been a long time since I've done this." He smiled down at her. "I wish we got more alone time don't you?"

She nodded but she cared less about those moments anymore. It was all about the dope and Gunner. "It feels nice when you brush my hair. Relaxing."

Lennon chuckled. "It may feel good now but at first you use to give me a hard time. Thought I would comb out your curls just because I added a little water. Ajax would have to come into the room and brush his own hair with water just to convince you things were fine." He shook his head. "You'd laugh when he took you into the bathroom next while he got into the shower with his clothes just to show you his curls bounce back."

Shayla laughed hysterically but stopped. She realized something was happening. "No, Dad-Ma." Her stare was cold. "You're not slick and I know what this is about."

He looked at her hair instead of focusing on her face. "All I'm doing is brushing your hair. Nothing is wrong."

She turned her head to look up at him. "You can't take him from me. I won't let you."

"I'm not doing anything, Shayla. You know I would never hurt you in that way. Still, you violated rule number one in the Ho Game. Never fall in love."

"But I—"

"Yesterday, when your friend came by I offered him Beverly since she just got out of jail. Ajax got her hair done, freshened her room with flowers and even had the housekeeper clean it from head to toe." He paused. "You know what your friend did? He turned

By T. Styles   229

her down. All he wants is you. Now I don't know if he realizes he's in love but I think he is."

Shayla stood up and walked across the room. "If you take him from me I'll die. I can't stand this life without him."

"What about the Prostitution Murders and all the crime that has gone on around here? Doesn't that bother you with this young man?"

Shayla swallowed the lump in her throat. "No...I trust him. I believe he will never hurt me so I'll—"

"He may look fresh, wear clean clothes and be easy on the eyes but at the end of the day he's still a John, Shayla. And he'll hurt you more than anyone else ever has because you care. Be warned."

"Okay."

"Okay what? That's all you have to say to me?"

"If he's taken from me your world will be hell." She glared. "Stay out of my way." She grabbed her brush. "And leave my fucking hair alone. Your fingers stink." She stormed to the bathroom and slammed the door.

CHAPTER EIGHTEEN
LENNON

Lennon walked into Ajax's office after getting a message from Beverly that he wanted to see him. He tied the belt on his red silk robe tighter and closed the door. He was smiling until Ajax turned around in the chair. The first thing Lennon noticed was the gold band around Ajax's wedding finger, which hadn't been there before.

Lennon, like the whores, heard rumors of him being with another woman but Lennon wanted, no…he *needed* desperately for it not to be true.

"You talk to Shayla?" Ajax asked, counting money behind the desk. "I went by her room earlier and she wasn't there."

Lennon stepped deeper into the room, his eyes on his finger. "Why are you…wearing that ring?" He pointed at it.

Ajax sat back in his large leather chair and it squeaked. "Did you find out anything on the boy? Like I asked?"

"So you aren't going to answer me?" Tears streamed down Lennon's face. "You gonna carry things like I don't matter? Like we haven't built a life together."

Seeing his tears, slowly Ajax rose and approached. Once in his face he slapped Lennon. "You know what your biggest problem is? Me." He pointed to himself.

Lennon shook his head no. "That's not true!"

Lennon backed into the wall while Ajax remained close, giving him no room to run. "When I needed you to bring in the girls I gave you the impression you meant more to me than you did. That you were my business partner. My equal." He paused. "That's it, right?"

"Ajax, don't—"

"SHUT THE HELL UP AND ANSWER MY QUESTION!"

"Ajax, please don't hit me again."

"Let me clear the air for you. Just like I fucked the rest of the girls to keep 'em in line you are no different."

Lennon held his stomach. "You don't mean that! It's just that...that you are around a lot of women. But...but I know you. You're a gay man who's had some insecurities in—"

"I'm not gay! I fucked them all, Lennon!" Ajax yelled in his face. "Even with me telling you, you still aren't listening. Which is why I didn't bother to tell you I got married in the first place." He paused. "But trust me when I say I had every girl in this house, even the ones that left."

"Please tell me you didn't touch…touch…my baby. Please tell me you didn't touch—"

"I especially fucked Shayla." Ajax grinned. "And trust me, I had her in every way possible."

Lennon flopped on the floor, the pain of his response too weighty to take on foot. "Why?" Lennon sobbed. "Why did you have to have her too? Why when you knew how much she meant to me? I manipulated her for you. Convinced her to sell her body all because I loved you and you kept questioning my loyalty. But it was all for nothing."

Ajax reached down, grabbed Lennon by the throat and squeezed. Lifting him up he took a deep breath and asked, "Did you find out anything on that boy? That's the only thing I want to talk about now."

Lennon looked him in the eyes and said, "No."

Ajax released him and Lennon coughed. "Well stay on him. I don't trust him and I will not let him destroy what I built." He pointed at him.

"What *you* built?" Lennon asked with wide eyes. "I was right here with you. The entire time. *We* built this! I gave my life for you and this place."

"That's because it belonged to me already." He said sarcastically.

Lennon took a deep breath and nodded. He was fed up with his shit. "Ajax, I'm not helping you anymore. If you want a flunky go get your wife."

Ajax laughed boisterously. "Now why would I do that when she has no idea what I do for a living?" He paused. "And why would I do that when I have you?"

Lennon wiped his tears. "Not my problem. You made me hate my own daughter ruined our relationship forever. Because of it I will never forgive you and I'm done with all of this."

Ajax laughed hysterically. "You're more delirious than I thought. So let me remind you who's king." He gripped his throat and hit him repeatedly in the center of the face with his five-finger ring.

Lennon's eyes were closed but it was the soft beeps that caused him to open them. When he awoke he was in a hospital.

He tried to speak but an oxygen cord going through his nostrils and into his throat pre-vented him from doing so. Ajax had beaten him into an extended hospital stay and he didn't even know the half.

The worst news was yet to come.

CHAPTER NINETEEN

SHAYLA

Shayla walked up and down the block with Kristy who stared at her for long periods of time like she was wearing another face. Finally, Shayla who couldn't take her side-glances anymore stopped walking and faced her. Crossing her arms over her chest she said, "What is it, Kristy? You annoying me right now."

Kristy placed her hands into her back pocket. "What you gonna do now?"

Shayla frowned. "I don't know what you talking about."

"Now that Lennon gone and only God knows where he at, what you gonna do? 'Cause you can't stay here."

Shayla shrugged. "How you know he gone?" She paused. "He probably just needed a little space from Ajax. And that cop who keep coming by asking questions."

"Beverly told me he's gone...and she said it may be for a long time too." She paused. "Anyway, did you know Ajax sent your friend away twice? Yesterday and today?"

Shayla's eyes widened. Up until that point she had assumed he'd forgotten about her like the others because she hadn't seen him in days. Hearing that he had actually made an attempt to reach her made her feel better. "Maybe he'll be back. He never listened to Ajax anyway."

"Not this time. He wants you to himself." She paused. "You should leave, Shayla." She moved closer to him. "If you can find him go and don't come back to this place. Maybe there's love for all of us. And if you find it maybe you can come back and tell me about it."

In hating mode, Beverly walked up to them with her hands on her hips. A small scar sat over her eye from where her face got banged into the John's car window and both girls loved it.

Sitting in silence she glared at them as if they were disobedient children. "Less talking and more searching." She clapped her hands together. "Look available ladies. You're not me but I'm sure somebody would want to fuck you." Beverly's glare fell on Kristy. "Or not."

"And who the fuck are you to tell us what to do?" Kristy asked.

"Who do you think I am?" Beverly grinned. "Come now, bitch, you know Ajax told me to check on you and that money. Let's not be foolish. Lennon is gone and I am in charge."

Just then a car pulled up to the women. Beverly picked at her curls while Kristy grinned heavily. It didn't matter what they did because it was Shayla who he wanted. "You available, Pretty Lady?" The John asked.

Embarrassed that he wasn't interested in her Beverly rolled her eyes. "Like I said make some money!" She stormed off.

Shayla cleared her throat. "Yes…I…"

Before she could respond fully Gunner's car pulled up to the curb and blocked the driver where he was parked. "Get in, Shayla."

Shayla was stuck.

The John looked out of his window at who was messing up his flow. When he saw Gunner he said, "Excuse me, but I was talking to her. Come back later if you—"

Gunner glared. "Am I talking to you, nigga?" He focused back on Shayla. "Get over here. Now."

"Wait a minute," the John persisted. "I said I was talking to her. You gonna have to — "

Fed up, Gunner pushed out of his car and stomped toward the John's vehicle. He pulled the door open and dragged the man to the ground. Once he was lying face up on the concrete Gunner kicked and punched him so much he passed out.

With his hand extended he walked up to Shayla. "Come with me. Don't make me ask again." She took his hand and jogged to the car.

They both got inside and pulled off, leaving tire tracks in their haste.

Shayla and Gunner walked into an upscale hotel in Washington DC. She was stunned as she looked around the luxurious room because she'd never been in any place so plush. Gunner on the other hand remained in the middle of the floor, arms behind his back observing her reactions. He'd been in these types of rooms all his life but it was nice feeling it through her expressions.

After she took in enough she turned around to face him. Suddenly she wasn't happy anymore and a frown covered her face. "I used to dream of coming to a place like this. Every time I watched a Hollywood movie.

"So what's the problem?"

"Why…why did you bring me here? To make me feel like trash for living how I've lived for so long? To show that you're better than me?"

He moved closer. "Tell me who you are."

She took a deep breath. "Who do you want me to be?"

"Shayla, tell me who you are. I want to know more."

Her heart rate increased just hearing him say her name. She looked around, walked to the sofa and plopped down. Everything in her spirit said she was out of her league.

What could she do?

Law of attraction had brought her the man of her dreams and she felt out of place and because of it she couldn't receive him. "I've never been asked that question before. Most people tell me who they want me to be and I conform."

He moved closer and sat next to her, their thighs touching lightly. "Okay...tell me something small. What you like to eat?"

She smiled. "I don't know."

"Where you want to visit? In the world?"

She shrugged. "I don't know."

He leaned back in his seat. "It's hard getting anything out of life when you don't know what you want." He paused. "Do you know what you want from me?"

Tears rolled down her cheeks. "Gunner, I don't know."

He nodded. "You been fucked up for a long time."

"Yes," she wiped the tears away. "Do you think I can...I can fix myself?" She reached into her purse and pulled out a bag of heroin. "I don't feel too well and I have to put my head on straight."

He frowned. "I don't want that shit around me."

"Well can I do it in the bathroom?"

"Whatever."

She rushed to the bathroom, closed the door and fifteen minutes later it opened and she leaned against the doorframe. High as a jet and more confident she grinned at him but he wasn't pleased. "You don't...don't like what you see do you?" Her words fell out lazily. "I'm ugly to you."

Silence.

"Then teach me how to be." She flopped next to him. "I'm lost and I'm asking you to show me the way. I need your...help." She paused and gazed at his face. Her stomach turned when she saw his expression grow cold. "Let me love you." She slid between his legs, removed his jeans and eased on top of him. He entered her pussy and she moaned. "You don't have to talk if you don't want. It's better like this anyway.

He grabbed the back of her head and pulled her into a deep kiss.

CHAPTER TWENTY

SHAYLA

Darkness covered the hotel room as Shayla lie in bed. It was the most sleep she'd gotten in a long time and she wanted to hold onto the peace and tranquility forever. So although she was awake, she didn't open her eyes...until she heard two men yelling outside the hotel like maniacs.

Curious about what was causing the racket, she pushed the curtain in the bedroom to the side only to see Gunner quarreling with another man next to a white car. They were yelling loudly and from her point of view she thought the man was Ajax.

This horrified her.

Trembling, she closed the curtains, backed into the wall and pressed both of her hands over her lips to muffle her cry. Ajax said there wasn't a place on earth she could run if she ever left and now she realized he was right. "What am I going to do? What am I going to do?" She kept chanting to herself.

She hoped the fighting would stop soon and he would go away but as the seconds ticked by the temperature of the dispute grew louder and more violent. Slowly she crept to the window and when she opened the curtains this time she saw Gunner's t-shirt was covered in blood.

She had to help him.

Even if it meant she had to help fight Ajax.

Her worst fear.

Walking away from the window like a mad woman she threw on her dress and looked around the room for a weapon. She walked up to a red glass lamp in the living room portion of the suite but it was bolted down to the table. It could be of no help.

"You wasting time," she told herself. "You gotta move now."

Taking a deep breath she ran out the door and toward the back of the hotel. By the time she got outside to the scene it was quiet and she saw Gunner stuffing the man into the trunk of his car. Stunned, she stopped walking and said, "Was...was that him?"

"Who?" His breaths were heavy.

"Ajax?" Her body trembled.

"What...no, Shayla." He slammed the trunk down in an effort to close it and looked around for witnesses. It stopped because the man's leg was hanging out. He pushed it back in, closed the trunk and said, "I promise you that wasn't him."

"Then what's going on, Gunner?"

"Just…just come here for a second," he said checking his surroundings every so often. She moved closer. "I need you to drive my car while I drive this one." He pointed to the vehicle that as of now was a moving coffin. "We have to —"

"I don't drive often." She paused. "Me and Bernice used to sneak Ajax's car out but I don't want to mess up yours."

"If you bang it up I'll get another one." He took the keys from his pocket and handed them to her. "You'll be fine." He was frantic and this was the first time she'd ever seen him lose cool. "I trust you."

"But what if the police catch me driving without a license? It's too early in the morning."

"Too early in the morning?" He paused. "What are you talking about?" Shaking his head he placed both palms on the sides of her face. "Please, Shayla. Do this for me. I need you right here and right now."

She nodded rapidly. "Okay…okay…" She swallowed. "I'll help."

An hour later, after Gunner dumped the coffin car in a ditch outside of Virginia, where cars seldom roam, he and Shayla were seated together in his ride driving back toward Maryland. She hadn't said a word so he looked over at her. "You okay?"

She nodded yes.

He sighed. "Look, that dude was gonna cause problems for me. He owed me some money and when he thought I was gonna kill him he turned informant. So I...I did what I had to do not to get locked up." He paused. "And you helped me."

"I'm not afraid of the murder. You do what you need to do in life to protect yourself. But I have to know something else about you, Gunner. And I need to know now."

He shook his head. "It's not that simple because—"

She pushed open the car door as Gunner drove down the highway. "What the fuck you doing?" She continued to try and get out of a moving car so he said,

"Okay...okay..." He pulled over. "Let me take you somewhere." She didn't seem too satisfied. "Please."

CHAPTER TWENTY-ONE

AJAX

Ajax smiled as he walked down the hallway of the hospital. He wore a black button down and matching slacks with fine red pinstripes. As he moved and gained all the attention he deserved, because his great looks concealed his evil ways, several women grinned and reddened as he walked by.

And yet he was on a mission.

Stepping up to the Patient Information Counter, he approached a thin white woman with stringy blonde hair. "I'm not gonna lie, you the finest thing I've seen all day," he said. "How are you, sexy?"

She covered her mouth and giggled into her fingers. Talking through her palm she said, "Better now."

"And that's what I like to hear, beautiful." He paused. "You see I have a dilemma. I'm looking for Lennon Holman. He here?"

"One second. I'll see if he's been admitted." After several clicks of her antiquated computer she said, "No...doesn't seem to be anyone here by that name."

Several more click-clacks filled the air.

"Nope...definitely no one here with that name." She looked up at him and grinned.

He frowned but smiled quickly to prevent her from being scared. He realized his ability to horrify women so he had to be easy to get what he wanted. Some information.

"Come on, sweetheart. Let's not start the day with you lying to me. He has to be here. Dropped him off myself. Found him on the side of the road." He looked around. "So don't fuck with me. Where is he?"

Her eyes widened as she took in the authority in his voice. Now she was afraid for her own life. If she said the wrong thing she could end up in a hospital bed like her patients. "Oh...yes...I...remember him."

"Good," he tapped the counter. "Now tell me where he is."

"I'm sorry, sir. But we aren't supposed to give out information on people under police protection. Maybe—"

He yanked her stringy hair and pulled her toward him. "Ouch!"

"Shut the fuck up, bitch," he said in her face. When she quieted down he looked around. One of the cute black girls who were interested in him also stopped short when she saw the violence against her co-worker. But when he winked at her she smiled and walked away. "Now tell me which room he's in our I'll gut you like a cow."

Lennon sipped apple juice threw a straw on the side of his mouth when Ajax strolled inside. He tried to move in an effort to stop further abuse but had long since lost the control of his legs, thanks to Ajax. He would now have to spend the rest of his days paralyzed from the waist down. And for a queen who loved a good shoe and great dancing, that was a hard fate to face.

With his arms behind his back, Ajax walked over to his bedside holding Polaroid pictures. "How are you?" When Lennon tried to reach for the red button alerting the staff that he needed help, Ajax removed it from him and dropped it to the floor. "Don't be rude...I asked how are you?"

Lennon's breath quickened. "What you doing here?"

"What do you mean? I came to check on you."

"Nurs—" Lennon attempted to scream but Ajax slammed his thick hand over his mouth, silencing and slapping him in the process. His teeth stabbed the inside of his upper lip and since the side of Ajax's palm was pressed against his nose he could smell the scent of a nasty woman.

"Nigga, I did you a favor." He said through clenched teeth. "I could've killed you. Instead I brought you to the hospital and saved your life." Ajax looked at the open doorway again. "Now you better show me some respect before I finish you off. Do you hear me?" He paused. "Now I'm gonna remove my hand and when I do you will show me some fucking respect or I will break your neck."

Lennon nodded slowly.

Ajax peeled his hand from his lips and Lennon licked them because his mouth was dry. "Now...I been thinking about what you said to me, about the boy who came for Shayla and I realized that your hate for me had you lying. Especially after I found these pictures." He tossed them on his stomach. "So I'll ask you again...what do you know about the kid?"

"Nothing."

Ajax stared him down for what felt like an hour although it was seconds. "You will give me everything you know on that boy and you will do it now."

"What happens if I don't?"

"I know things about your precious daughter. A lot of things and I'll be sure you go down with her."

"Like what?" He said through heavy voices.

"Let's just say I've collected a lot of horror stories over the months. And I'm about to tell you two of 'em."

Shayla, Gunner and Max, Gunner's friend, were eating breakfast on Max's deck in Virginia. As they looked out into his backyard the woods that surrounded his property seamed to show off the sun as it rose slowly and seductively.

The atmosphere was perfect, not to mention they were stuffed and relaxed. Two hours earlier Gunner called Max and told him he was bringing a friend. His comrade was excited. A chef to his core, and always looking to show off for the ladies, he prepared a breakfast cuisine worthy of his popular restaurant in Georgetown.

When the meal was consumed they talked about life, people and the pursuit of happiness. Shayla was surprised at how great of a time she was having because in the past she didn't feel worthy being around well off people. It was then that she realized that the skills she developed that were necessary to make men happy translated through life. All she had to do was engage and notice people and they would fall to her feet.

"So, Shayla, tell me about yourself," Max said as he leaned back in his chair and rubbed his belly. A toothpick rested in the small of his back teeth. "And don't hold back."

Shayla crossed her legs and placed her hands on her thighs. "Uh...what you want to know?"

"Anything you wanna tell me." He grabbed his Mimosa and took a large gulp. "Been a long time since my man has brought a beautiful young lady to meet me. So I'm curious about you."

"Go 'head, man," Gunner said. "Stop it."

"I'm serious," Max continued.

Shayla looked at Gunner who smiled and shook his head. He didn't seem uncomfortable about his friend prying so she decided to loosen up. If he didn't care that she was a whore she wouldn't care either. "Well, let's just say I've made a life out of making people happy."

Max nodded. "Wow... sounds interesting."

"It is, and when I think about it, I do exactly what you do." She wiped her hair from her face. "I heard somewhere that food is the window of the soul so you can say what I do is like...well...the back door."

Gunner laughed and rubbed her thigh while Max chuckled. "Your friend sounds like a winner."

Gunner nodded. "I hope so." He stood up. "But let me go piss right quick. I be back."

When he excused himself Max looked in the direction he walked into and waited for him to disappear. Suddenly he seemed on edge and his pleasant disposition vanished. "Where you meet him from?"

Her eyebrows rose. "Why? What's wrong?"

"I asked you a fucking question," Max said through clenched teeth. "Now where you meet him from?"

She wasn't feeling the heat he was bringing her way so she said, "Maybe you should ask him instead."

He sat back in his seat. "Have it your way. But I think it's a good idea to let you know your life is in danger. I'ma leave it at that."

Ajax sat in his car, across the street from where Lennon said he last saw Gunner go some time back. Although Lennon didn't want to part with the information he knew about Gunner, because he wanted Shayla to live, he was more concerned for his own life since Ajax was standing over his bed looking like Jason Vorhees. In the end he felt it best to break off the information he knew.

And so there Ajax sat. Waiting. And plotting.

Within an hour a young girl and an older woman walked out the house. Ajax slid down a little to be hidden behind his steering column until he was ready to be seen. When the younger girl came back out alone he felt now was the time to make his move. He pushed out of his car and rushed toward her. Wearing his smile he said, "Hey, young lady, can I talk to you for a moment?"

She nodded, raised the lid to the iron trashcan and dumped the bag inside. "That depends, 'cause I'm not 'spose to talk to strangers." She crossed her arms over her chest. "What you want to know?"

"Well you know a friend of mine and I wanted to ask you a few questions."

The girl looked him over. Something in her spirit said not to trust him. "Maybe I should go in the house."

Ajax grabbed her arm and maintained his hold. "Please don't leave. I came here in good will. You don't have to be afraid of me."

She looked at his hand. "Can you get off me? Please."

He released her and placed his hands behind his back. "Done...now..." he took a deep breath. "What do you know about Gunner?"

She frowned. "What's there to know about him?"

"I take it by your mood that you hate him more than you do me in this moment." He laughed softly. "Am I right?"

"I can't stand him. He's ruined my life and I will never forgive him for the things he did to me. Ever."

Ajax nodded. "Well, it seems like we have found a common enemy."

She crossed her arms over her chest again. "If that's what you want to call it."

"I do." He paused. "So what kind of relationship do you two have?"

"He stops by once a week and drops off money." She paused. "Other than that there's not much to report."

Ajax's eyebrows rose. "Wow, sounds to me like you should like the guy. Especially if he giving you cash money."

"Well I don't."

He looked up and down the expensive neighborhood. "I get it...I get it." He paused. "So tell me, when you expect him back?"

"Later today." Suddenly she smiled. "Why you gonna hurt him or something? Because if you did, that would be okay with me."

Ajax laughed. "I bet it would."

CHAPTER TWENTY-TWO
SHAYLA

Gunner and Shayla walked down the mall with so many bags neither could carry another if someone gave it to them for free. When they got to the car he tossed the bags in the trunk and then his backseat. On the road again she looked over at him and said, "I can't believe how they smell."

He grinned. "How what smells?"

"The clothes. They smell different than the stuff I'm used to."

He nodded. "It's the new smell." He paused. "That's the first odor I fell in love with. And the cause of me moving dope." He maneuvered the car a little more in silence. "Well...part of it."

"So that's what you do?"

He winked.

She looked to her left and then at him. "Thank you. I don't know what your reason is for doing all of this but...thank you." She sighed. "Nobody has ever treated me so nice. I feel like a princess or something."

"If you don't know what my reason is by now I'm doing something wrong."

"What does that mean?" She shrugged. "I barely know anything about you. I mean...what's going on between us?"

"All I can say is that I like something about you. And I want you comfortable when we go out so I got you new gear."

"But I was comfortable before the new clothes."

"No you weren't." He shook his head. "You stay tugging at them little ass dresses to bring them down over your thighs. Only to have the crack of your ass hanging out in the back. I want you to know that dealing with me means shit ain't got to be like it used to be."

She wiped her hair out her face. "Do you always...pick up girls and stuff?" She paused. "Is it your thing to make ho's dreams come true?"

He chuckled. "I have no idea what you mean."

"Like...do you pick up prostitutes all the time and do this kind of stuff?"

He chuckled harder. "Nah..."

"Nah...that's all you got to say? I'm serious. Please answer my question."

He shrugged. "Look, I've already done more talking around you than I have with anybody." He took a deep breath. "Recently anyway." He looked at her. "Even if I did pick up chicks in the past if I'm kicking it with you now what difference does the rest make?"

"A lot. To me." She paused. "I spent almost everyday of my life being like everybody else. I need to feel different. I need to feel like I'm the only one you do this for or else everything anybody else has said to me is true. That I'm not worthy of anything. And I—"

"We got one more stop to make." He winked at her. "Let me see how you feel after that."

Gunner pulled up to a large suburban home in Reisterstown Maryland. Made of brick, the sturdy home looked like it belonged to a superstar and she wondered who lived inside the abode.

As if it were nothing, Gunner pulled a remote off his visor and activated the alarm. Immediately the two-car garage doors rose quietly and he eased inside the available space, next to a red Mercedes Benz. When it closed again they were in partial darkness.

Once parked he looked over at her. "Don't worry about the bags. I'll get the stuff later."

She opened the door and they both walked into the side door leading into the house. The large cathedral ceilings, the state of the art appliances in the kitchen and living room blew her away. It was breathtaking. "Gunner...who lives here? Some kind of lawyer or doctor or something?" She was in total awe.

"I live here."

Her jaw dropped and she faced him. "No you don't...stop playing."

He chuckled. "I do."

Gently, she walked toward a brass living room table, which held four pictures in gold frames. She raised one of a beautiful older woman and viewed it closely. "Who is this?"

He opened the refrigerator and brought her a bottle of water and looked at what she was presenting. "Oh...that's my mother."

Shayla observed the picture again. "She's beautiful." She paused. "Where is she now?"

"Dead." His response was cold and he grabbed her hand. She sat the picture down before taking a seat on the sofa. "A long time ago."

She twisted the cap off the water and looked around again. "I can't believe how...how pretty it is here." She paused. "You have to tell me who you are, Gunner. You took me to a fancy hotel, introduced me to your rich friend and now you bring me here. Oh, let me not forget about the body in the trunk of—"

He frowned and grabbed her arm forcefully. "That never fucking happened." She seemed confused and he squeezed harder. "Do you hear me? That never happened. Say it."

She nodded. "That never happened."

He released her and she rubbed her throbbing arm. "Good, I brought you here so you can see there's something about you I like. And for a nigga like me that has to be enough."

His phone rang. "Give me a second." He reached over and answered. "Hello." Quickly he leapt up, fear pained across his face. "Where are you?" He paused. "I'm on my way." He hung up

"Something wrong?" Shayla asked.

"We have to take another ride. I'm sorry."

GUNNER

Gunner positioned the pillow behind Lisa's head as she got situated in the hospital bed. When he was done ensuring she was comfortable, he observed the bruises on her face. A strange man, who she had yet to identify, struck her so many times she was almost unrecognizable. Red bruises surrounded by black knots were everywhere.

Gunner stood next to her, unsure of what to say. "I'm sorry about this, Lisa." He looked into her eyes. "I don't know who —"

"Why is it that everything you do causes me pain?" She yelled. "Why can't you stay out my life?"

"How do you know this is my fault?" He paused. "And you know I can't stay out of your life."

"Why not?" She cried. "You a drug dealer and I don't want you around. What's so hard to understand?"

Gunner sat in a chair next to the bed. "I hear you but I care about you, Lisa."

"Who cares what you want! All I want is for you to leave me alone."

"You my daughter!" He yelled. "That's why I won't leave you! And after what happened to your mother I...I can't. You can hate me all you want but when you need me I will be there."

"Why? So I can die like you killed my mother?"

"Don't say—"

"You beat my mother to death! It's because of you I don't have her and now you're ruining my life too." She sobbed uncontrollably. "Just go."

"Lisa, I—"

"GO!"

He stood up and walked toward the bed. Her back was in his direction as his hand hovered over her leg, stopping short of touching her. "At least tell me who came over my sister's house and did this? What was his name? Because I know you know."

Silence.

"Lisa...can you at least tell me who did this to you?"

"He said to tell you his name was Ajax."

Gunner was so angry he shivered. The fact that he laid hands on his daughter had him on some murderous shit...again. How did he even know where he lived? He took a deep breath and walked out.

In a zombie gait, Gunner was halfway down the hallway when he glanced to his right and saw Lennon in a hospital bed. Confused, he walked into his room. "Don't I know you?" Gunner looked around to see if anybody was in earshot. "From the spot."

Lennon's eyes widened at first but then he nodded his head. "Yes, and I'm actually glad you found me."

Gunner stomped up to his bed. "My kid in a room here on account of Ajax. How he know where my daughter lived?"

Lennon took a deep breath. "I followed you one day." He paused. "But I knew where you lived a long time ago. And at first I didn't give him the address but after what he did to me," he looked down at himself, "well...you can understand my position."

Gunner wiped his hand down his face. "He beat my kid to the point where I almost didn't recognize her. No offense but you a grown man. She's a kid. What's up with ya'll niggas? It's gotta be deeper than pussy."

"Have a seat."

"I asked a question!"

"Sit down, Gunner, Please."

Gunner flopped into a chair next to his bed just as a nurse walked into the room in a hurry. "Is everything okay?" She questioned Lennon. "We were alerted that something was wrong in your room."

Lennon forgot he hit the button. His nerves were on edge. "Yes." He paused. "It was an accident."

She smiled and walked out.

"Tell me what's up," Gunner said seriously.

"This is all about Shayla...my daughter." He sighed. "Well she isn't my real daughter but I raised her and loved her all the same."

"Where did she come from?"

"Ajax, well, he stole her."

"What the fuck? From where?"

"I don't know where but I do know it was from her mother when she was two years old. He said he gave her to me because I'd always wanted children when for real it was all a game to make her a...to make her a..."

"Whore." Gunner said.

Lennon nodded. "I helped at first because the drugs had me messed up. My thoughts stayed clouded in this relationship. But if I had known what he would turn her into today I would've never participated."

"So it's your fault she sells her body?"

"Gunner...oh, Gunner...its much deeper than that now."

CHAPTER TWENTY-THREE

SHAYLA

Shayla exited a cab and walked to Max's house. She carried an orange MCM purse and was wearing a black cat suit that Gunner bought for her. Her current gear was a long road from her whorish days and she felt more comfortable, more accepted.

When Gunner got the call earlier from Lisa that she was in danger, he dropped Shayla off at the hotel and told her he'd return later. Needing to know more about the man she met at breakfast and the weird warning he delivered she went in search of answers.

Shayla knocked on his front door and after five minutes Max opened it and frowned when he saw her face. "What you doing here?" He looked over her head for Gunner's car.

"You wanted to talk to me when we were here before." She paused. "Can you talk to me now?"

He looked around and ran his hand down his face. "I said all I needed to say so—"

"Please." She moved closer. "I'm begging you."

He observed her modest clothing. "Come in, I'll make us some coffee."

Ten minutes later they were seated in the living room with past newspaper articles of women beaten in recent and past years. In addition he had present articles of men murdered.

"What are you showing me?" She asked.

"I think Gunner may be responsible for this."

She scratched her scalp. "But...why would you say that?"

Max took a deep breath. "First what did he tell you about his past?"

"Nothing...which is why I'm here."

He shook his head. "Gunner was married once. When I tell you I never saw his eyes light up for a woman before, I mean exactly what I say. To tell you the truth I didn't think it could ever happen again." He focused on Shayla. "And then he met you."

"Go ahead," she said softly. "Please."

"Anyway, eventually his wife, who he wasn't married to at the time, got pregnant. And he still didn't know anything about her life before him. Stuff like where she came from, who her family was or even where she lived." He paused. "I guess he was tired of females on the street because before I knew it he married her." He sighed. "Things were going good until he discovered his cousin Leon hired the girl for his birthday. As a joke." He paused again. "Leon thought the situation was over that same night of his birthday. I mean, everybody figured that at the very least he would get a divorce but their relationship continued."

"So she was a prostitute?"

"Yes."

"But...but how didn't he know?"

"I gotta back up some." He paused. "First let me say Gunner wasn't the type of cat to sleep with chicks for money. I mean look at the kid," He chuckled.

"But why did they trick him with a prostitute?"

"Leon always been a jealous cat. And like I said Gunner was never the type of guy who had to pay to play." He paused. "Anyway Leon knew that in order to get him to fall for Selena, which was her name, he had to think he met her on his own.

"So he set up this elaborate scene at his birthday party where she walked in with three other pretty whores and one thing led to another. They fell for each other had a little girl and everything. But Leon got locked up and forgot to tell Gunner it was all a joke."

"He has a daughter?"

He nodded yes."

She cleared her throat because for some reason the news hurt. She didn't want him attached at all. "So...why is that a bad thing?" She shrugged.

"It wasn't a bad thing until recently his mother needed a blood transfusion. She fell in a pool and busted her head, lost a lot of blood." He paused. "But to see if he was a match he got tested and received a positive reading. "

"Positive? What's that?"

"Come on, you had to have heard about the virus HIV that's going around?" He paused. "The one Magic Johnson said he contracted a couple years ago."

Shayla recalled hearing about that in the news and her stomach buckled. She realized her lifestyle was dangerous but she never assumed she'd get anything until that moment. "So...so he's positive? Does that mean he can die?"

"People still trying to learn about this disease. Let's just say we thought it was a death sentence at the time." He paused. "And what did he do? Questioned Selena about her lifestyle. She told him she was a prostitute and that Leon hired her and everything. Shit was worse when his mother died days later."

Shayla sighed. "Wow." She paused. "But how do you get the disease?"

He shrugged. "I'm not sure just like you. But after hearing different stories in the news she assumed she gave it to him." He paused. "And on that night he beat her into a coma. With his fists. The thing was she was pregnant again."

Shayla stood up. "How far along?"

"Far enough." He paused. "But that's the weird part nobody could figure out. His daughter stayed alive in Selena's womb even though she wasn't conscious. So they kept her on life support until the baby was born, thinking they could save the infant. The next morning Selena died on her own. The baby died two days later." He sat back. "So that's Selena, the baby and his mother gone all at once."

"Oh my God."

"I know but that's not the worst. Days after his kid died prostitutes started showing up missing and dead."

"You don't think he would—"

"All I know is he was hurt. He was hurt that his cousin would set him up and hurt that he fell for her. Add to all of this his baby girl died and later his mother." He shook his head. "If you ask me, as mad as he was, I think he may have been responsible for all those deaths and even the ones in the news now."

Shayla cried. "I'm so...so confused. I...don't think he's capable."

"Then you're wrong." He pointed at her. "About six months after Selena died, he came to my house one day. I was getting married to this chick I thought I loved." He waved the air. "Wrong move but he was telling me how he wished he had true love. And how many people would be alive that day if Leon never played that joke."

"But what does that mean?"

"A lot...for starters his cousin Leon showed up missing and like I said people started dropping like flies." He paused. "It wasn't until I told him he should get re-tested that he thought about another option."

"Did he?"

"Yes." He sat back. "He was negative. Turns out he didn't have HIV. There was a mix-up at the doctor's office between his blood sample and another man's."

Shayla gasped. "What happened?"

"The prosecutors waited while Selena was still on life support. When she died they charged him with murder for her death. But on some freakish shit he ended up beating it on a technicality." He moved closer. "But after that he was reckless. Fighting for no reason, fucking anything that moved and the next thing I know you came in the picture."

She stood up. "I have to...I have to leave. I'm sorry."

"Shayla!" He yelled. "Don't tell him I told you these things!"

She rushed toward the door and ran down the street. Once she made it to the end of the block she leaned on her knees and tried to catch her breath. Everything she learned was so overwhelming and she didn't know how to process it all.

When she began to walk again Ajax pulled up on her. "Get in, Shayla. Don't make me chase you."

CHAPTER TWENTY-FOUR
GUNNER

Gunner entered the hotel suite exhausted. After dealing with Lisa, child protective services and Lennon the last thing he wanted to do was to tell Shayla he didn't need the drama in his life. But it had to be done and it had to be done right away because he wanted zero baggage before he killed Ajax.

"Shayla, where you at?" He yelled as he walked to the refrigerator. He removed a water bottle twisted the cap and took a big gulp. "Shayla, come out here for a second. We have to talk."

When he didn't see her he walked into the bedroom and saw the bed was made which meant housekeeping entered. Still she was nowhere to be found. So he marched to the bathroom and banged on the closed door with his knuckles.

"Shayla, you in there? I gotta talk to you right now."

When she didn't reply he pushed his way inside. Like the rest of the suite it was empty and clean but there was a note on the closed toilet lid. He picked it up, walked out and sat on the edge of the bed to read it.

Gunner I can't see you anymore. You have too much going on. Please don't come looking for me. Go on with your life.

He looked at the letter once more, balled it up and tossed it in the trash.

"Fuck!" He paused. "I should've never dealt with that stupid bitch. Like I ain't got enough problems as is!"

When the hotel phone rang he rushed toward it. "Hello."

"They're releasing me from the hospital today," Lisa said with an attitude. "I need you to come pick me up."

"I'm on my way."

Gunner ambled through the hospital hallway to scoop his daughter when he ran into Lennon who was seated in a wheel chair with a nurse pushing him down the corridor. When Gunner walked by he grabbed his hand. "Gunner, can I talk to you for a minute?"

He snatched away from him. "This ain't my problem no more. Your girl left so I'm staying out of this shit."

"Please…just for one minute."

Gunner looked at his watch. "Yeah, aight."

Lennon looked up at the nurse who smiled and walked away. "Do you mind pushing me to my room?"

Gunner, annoyed at everything, he pushed the wheelchair to the room for privacy. At first he shoved it so hard Lennon almost banged into the wall. "What, man? I gotta pick up my daughter so I can't stay long."

"Ajax got Shayla. I called today to check on her and got a hold of Kristy instead. Gunner, I know you mad but you have to help her. Please."

"This ain't my —"

"Please, Gunner! I'm begging you or else she will die!"

He took a deep breath. "Okay…but first you have to tell me everything."

CHAPTER TWENTY-FIVE
GUNNER

Soft voices could be heard upstairs as Gunner walked into the basement of the brothel. Broken glass from the window he'd smashed crunched under his feet. With each step on the stairs leading upward the wood creaked lightly, whispering of the intruder's existence. His gun was cocked and loaded while sitting firmly in his palm. With each stride that led to his ascend he could see the wooden door necessary to enter the brothel come into view.

Focused, he crept upwards, the steps groaning louder, until he happened upon the closed door.

Once there he turned the knob slowly and pushed it open. When he saw a whore and her John entering a room, he closed it slightly and peeked out of the small slit. When they disappeared he eased into the hallway briskly until he reached Ajax's office.

Opening the door he saw Ajax was seated behind his desk with Beverly next to him. Wasting zero time Gunner fired at his arm, hitting him instantly. Blood gushed from the wound as Ajax screamed and jumped up.

"Sit down!" Gunner yelled. "I mean it!" Slowly he took a seat as Gunner haphazardly shook the gun. "You, sit the fuck down too!" He yelled at Beverly. When she was too afraid to move he grew louder. "I SAID SIT THE FUCK DOWN!"

Beverly sat on the floor and Gunner walked deeper inside the office, closing the door behind himself.

Ajax smiled slyly, while holding his wounded arm. "Wow, always knew her pussy was worth gold but I never thought you'd go this far. Look at yourself. You ready to die for a Ho."

"That gash gonna bleed out soon." Gunner said waving his gun crazily. "So you better tell me where she is so you can tend to it and then go back to whatever the fuck you were doing."

Ajax nodded. "Have a seat. I'll—"

"Where the fuck is she?" Gunner screamed louder. "I ain't come here to talk about nothing! Or to have no seats! Where is she?"

"I'm gonna tell you where she is but first I wanna tell you something about your innocent, precious woman. Something you need to know before you take her up out of here and save the day."

"The only thing you better be telling me is her location. Time running out and I'm about to shoot you someplace permanent."

Ajax nodded. "You still feel that way? Even if Shayla is a serial killer?"

Gunner chuckled. "What…what you talking about? You'd do anything to keep me from taking her out of here. Been trying since the first day you met me."

"I'm telling you the truth, young blood." He pointed at him with a bloody finger before touching his wound again. "I'm on my way out of state right now because she has killed many. Everybody in this brothel knows it too." He looked to the right. "Even Beverly."

"Liar!" Gunner yelled pointing the gun at him.

"Have you heard of the Prostitution Murders?"

"Yeah…so what?"

"Well, what you don't know is that when I didn't let Shayla leave she decided to sabotage me from behind the scenes. Killing my customers…thinking I would change my mind." He laughed. "But you can tell she never knew me. As many cats as I killed in these streets? Fuck I care if she offs one Kerb Crawler or two? But then another and another followed."

Gunner paced the area in front of his office. "This...this not making sense." He scratched his scalp.

Ajax laughed. "I'm telling you that she killed five of my regular customers. Maybe more." He shrugged, hand still on his bleeding wound.

"Why you beat my daughter the way you did?" He yelled, approaching the desk even more. "What part of the game is that?"

"You not gonna believe this either but it was her idea. She knew if I beat her that you would come." He laughed. "Don't know what you did to her but she hates you. Looking for a way to get you caught up. Maybe get the law involved." Ajax lowered his voice when he realized Gunner wasn't getting the joke. "My only objective was for you to let Shayla go, man. I needed my eyes on her at all times. When I helped her clean up some of her crimes my name was all over it. She gets caught I do too. And I couldn't have that."

"Where is she?" He asked as his nostrils flared.

Ajax laughed harder. "Don't you see? My getting Shayla away was not for her, but for you. I'm doing you a favor by taking her away from you."

"Where is she, man? I'm getting tired of asking."

He frowned. The boy would not relent. "Do you really think I will let you leave here with her? After everything I invested? She's coming with me to Atlanta and I—" Gunner shot him in the middle of the head and then popped Beverly in the throat.

He waited to be sure they died and afterward walked out.

Shayla sat in the mirror drugged up from heroin, courtesy of Ajax. She was preparing for her next customer when the door flew open. It was Gunner. "Get up, Shayla."

She shook her head, tears rolled down her face. "No...just leave me. I deserve to be here." She stood up. "And I don't want him to hurt you."

"Look, I ain't gonna be here all day." He glanced at the door and back at her. "Get up. We have to go now."

"You don't understand, Gunner. My life is too complicated…It's too…" She took a deep breath. "Too much."

Gunner considered her for a moment because something told him to go the other way but he couldn't leave her alone. Had he just been there for Selena instead of blaming an illness on her she didn't have, she would be alive and his daughter wouldn't hate him so much.

"Shayla, I don't know everything that happened in your life. But you were taken from your mother, thrown into prostitution and ain't been right since." He wiped his hand down his face. "This ain't really none of my business but look… I'm here ready to help you but you gotta move now. Don't make me change my mind."

Gunner and Shayla were lying in bed facing one another in his house. "Thank you," she said quietly. "For…everything."

He winked. "Feel better?"

She nodded. "Some but I think I gotta get away from here." She paused. "Maybe go some place where nobody knows me. Some place I can get clean." She looked into his eyes and her face grew serious. "So you...killed him? Ajax?"

"Don't ask me that again." He paused. "I said he's gone and that's all you need to know."

She nodded. "I know you have a daughter and had a wife and another baby that died." His eyes widened and he sat up in bed. "Your friend told me."

He exhaled. "That dude always running his mouth." He sighed.

"So it's not true?" She paused. "Because I think you wanted him to tell me. So you wouldn't have to."

"Believe what you want." He paused. "And I do have a kid and I should've handled her a little differently, she's just a child and none of it was her fault. I'm trying to make amends." He sighed. "Maybe even have her talk to somebody but how you go about that when you don't trust niggas?" He stood up and placed his t-shirt over his head. "We going somewhere so get dressed."

"Where?"

"You trust me?"

"I do."

"Well that should be enough."

Shayla sat in an elegant restaurant with Gunner but she felt something was off with his mood. For starters he was acting jittery and instead of being sent to a table for two it was set up for three. Sensing her nervousness he touched the top of her hand. "Don't be afraid."

She grabbed the white cotton napkin off the top of the table and placed it on her lap, twisting it in knots on both ends. "I don't understand what this is about." She glanced around. "Are you expecting somebody else?"

"You'll see."

Within fifteen minutes and three tequila shots later for Shayla, a beautiful woman walked inside of the restaurant. From the doorway she gazed around the establishment and smiled when her eyes fell on Shayla.

She was familiar to Shayla as Shayla tried to remember where she'd seen her face. Had her life not been so hard since their last meeting the moment she met her would've been recalled quicker in her mind.

Finally she looked over at Gunner and said, "Who is she?"

The woman sat in the available seat.

"Your mother," Gunner said.

She was rocked emotionally.

Shayla glanced at the beautiful woman again and observed her closely. Her hair, now grey was swept in a bun on top of her head but her face, although 52 in age held zero wrinkles. And her eyes were the brightest Shayla had ever seen in her life.

"Hello, Kaysa," Louise said softly, tears streaming down her cheeks. "I prayed for this moment."

"I saw you somewhere."

Louise smiled. "Try hard, you'll remember."

Shayla, trembling, sat across from Louise and finally she felt gut punched. "You…the…grocery store. I saw you that day in the grocery store." She felt nauseous and placed her hand on her belly to calm down.

Gunner stood up. "I'm gonna leave ya'll alone."

By T. Styles   287

"No!" Shayla grabbed his wrist. She looked up at him. "Please stay. I need you here."

Gunner slowly sat back down and held her hand under the table. Louise reached over and touched Shayla's other hand but she snatched it away. "Kaysa—"

"Shayla!" She said angrily. "My entire life my name has been Shayla. Every time I cried myself to sleep my name was Shayla. Every time I gave oral sex for money my name had been Shayla and every time I was raped my name has been Shayla! It's not about to change now because my no good ass mother came into view."

Gunner squeezed her hand slightly to calm her down. She looked at him and he whispered, "It's okay."

Slowly Shayla's head rotated to Louise." How did you find me?"

"Lennon...he...he reached out to me." Louise paused. "Told me where to find Gunner." She paused. "I have no idea what you've been through but I'm so sorry. I was a young girl when I had you and you were stolen from me. But you right...I wasn't a good mother." She paused. "And I'm sad to say that I didn't deserve a child because I wasn't in the right frame of mind. I was on drugs and…and I abandoned you way before that monster stole you from me."

Shayla wiped the tears away with her fist. "Well, what if I don't need you no more? What if I'm good now?"

Louise placed her hand over hers again. "Every girl needs her mother. EVERY GIRL."

"What's gonna happen with Lennon?" Shayla exhaled. "Since Ajax kidnapped me? I guess you gonna press charges."

"Well," she took a deep breath, "Lennon has agreed to tell the authorities what happened and since Ajax was killed tonight by someone, he's already taken care of." Louise exhaled. "But Shayla, there's something else."

Shayla's eyes widened because she couldn't take on any more news. This was all too much. "What is it now?"

"The police has some questions for you about some murders in Baltimore."

Shayla released Gunner's hand and clasped her palms together on the table. "What murders? I ain't do nothing."

"Apparently Ajax sent a letter to a Detective Johnson before he died." She paused. "He was leaving for Atlanta before he was murdered but told her that you had everything to do with the Prostitution Murders in the news." She paused. "Even told her where to find the bodies."

"What bodies?" Shayla asked.

"Sweetheart, it's over," Louise said. "No need to lie anymore. Now we gotta come up with a plan."

"But I didn't do anything," She continued.

"Shayla," Louise said more firmly. "It's over."

Slowly the expression changed from fear to anger. She looked at Gunner and then Louise. "So what if I did?"

"It doesn't matter if you did. We saying the same thing, Shayla," Gunner said. "I got a lawyer for you. A good one. But if it's gonna work you have to get in front of these crimes."

"And I'll be there when you get out," Louise said.

"Me too," Gunner added. "The most you'll do is some short time in a mental institution. I'll see to that."

Louise sighed, leaned closer and whispered, "There's so much I want to tell you but I'll start here."

Louise took a deep breath. "The day I found out I was pregnant, I killed a man too." She whispered.

Shayla looked at Gunner who wiped his hand down his mouth.

"And from what I'm told by people who knew my mother, she killed too," Louise continued. "Many men."

Shayla's stomach twirled. "What about my father? Was he...sane?"

Louise sat back in her seat. "I met him on the stroll, Shayla. I knew he loved me but he hated me for it too. And to answer your question at some point he tried to take my life." She paused and rolled up her sleeve to show the mark on her arm where Hiro stabbed her. "So you see, it ain't just you, Shayla. The thing you, me, your daddy and my mama had in common was the absence of love and I'm here now to help with that." She paused. "Well...I'm gonna leave you two alone. But I'll call Gunner tomorrow to see what you decide. No matter what I'm still gonna be there." Louise stood up and shook Gunner's hand. "I'm glad she found you. I prayed for someone like you in my life but never found it." She walked away.

Gunner moved his chair closer. "Talk to me about something else, Gunner. Anything to get my mind off of this."

He nodded. "Well, I'm a dope boy who opened a few pizza shops on the side. Made a lot of money...still making it now." He paused "Other than that I care about you. A lot."

She looked into his eyes. "I'm scared."

"I know."

"What if they don't let me out? Of the mental house?"

He glanced around and leaned back. "From what I found out they only have you on two bodies. Don't cop on anything else even if you did it. Your mother is gonna testify that you were kidnapped at a young age. And you were a teenager when these dudes were jumping on you. Who wouldn't be fucked up with a life like that? It's gonna work." He paused "Trust me."

"But you haven't been through anything like this. I'm talking murder."

He grabbed her face. "I killed three prostitutes before." He released her. "Before I found out I was HIV negative I was gonna kill you. It was on the first day I met you. When you sucked my dick off top." He shook his head and smiled. "For some reason I couldn't do it even though it was my plan."

Shayla was already armed with the information, courtesy of his friend but she wanted him to tell her more. "So why didn't you kill me?"

"I was gonna come back and finish you off. But I found out I was negative and wanted to have you again." He took a deep breath. "One thing led to another and…now I'm here."

"Wow," she said softly.

"I know it's fucked up." He said. "But I'm telling you this because I want you to know that you will get away with it. Just like me."

She trembled and her faced reddened upon hearing the news. His friend was right. "You're just like me," she said.

"That's right and I'll kill anybody who tries to get in the way of us."

Her eyes twinkled. "Don't leave me. If I go in don't leave me please."

"I will be there when you get out." He said firmly "Nobody will keep me away from you."

Shayla looked outwards as if she were daydreaming. "I want to tell you about two of the murders. About what happened when I killed them." She glanced at him. "Are you ready to hear the stories?"

He sat back in his seat. "Yes."

She stared outward again. "The first one was on the day Bernice hung herself. That night she was scheduled with Lyle and he was so mean, Gunner. So mean and angry. Like the devil or something." She paused. "And even though I wasn't speaking to her because she betrayed me, I didn't want her to have to deal with Lyle again. I didn't want my worst enemy to have him."

Gunner nodded. "Tell me more."

THE NIGHT SHAYLA KILLED LYLE

Lyle sat on the edge of Bernice's bed, naked from the waist down. With his dick nestled between her lips, she went to work pleasuring him, hoping he wouldn't be violent if she satisfied his sick needs.

With his hand on the gold wig on her head he said, "Keep it right there before I fuck you up out here." His tongue hung out the side of his lips like he was dying of thirst. "I swear that shit feels right."

"You got it, Lyle," she said as she ran her tongue around the tip of is sticky penis. "I told you I would be better this time. So you won't have to get mad at me."

"Yeah you told me that shit but I ain't cum yet," he pushed his penis in harder, hoping to gag her. "You got me going crazy." He pumped wildly and she took each blow like it was nothing.

When it started to feel too good, he pushed her back with a shove to the forehead. He wanted sex and pain. "Get on the bed. I want to do that other thing."

Horrified, she shook her head no. "Please don't make me do it, Lyle. It always hurts." She crawled on the bed.

"You can take it...stop fucking around." He slid off the mattress and grabbed one of the drumsticks he kept on him since he played in a band. Next he crawled on the bed and slapped her legs open. "Aight...here it comes."

He pushed the stick in and out of her vagina despite the screaming and blood while begging him to stop. When she appeared to be in immediate pain he jumped on top of her to be rough. Lyle was the type of nigga who couldn't cum unless he was causing pain.

Little did he know, danger was near.

The thin mattress squealed under her fragile body and the cheap gold wig she had been forced to wear caused the sides of her cheeks to itch, which summoned a smooth lumpy rash around her angelic face.

Opening her eyes a little, through the rough curls she could see his scowl as he pounded at her flesh, not caring that this moment, like the others, would only add to the nightmares that would torment her life. He had paid for her and he was determined to get his money's worth no matter how violent.

"You like that girl?" He asked, as the weight of his 220-pound body continued to press into her 110-pound frame. "Because I know you like it, now let me hear you tell me." He licked her face, his rough tongue scraping at her jaw.

She smiled a little like she had been taught and nodded rapidly. "Yes...it's...it's nice."

"Good," he smirked, his thrusts slowing in an attempt to make the moment last. "Because you got a future in the business, don't let anybody tell you any different. Unlike some of these bitches you can take dick. That's one thing for sure."

She slammed her eyes closed. "Thank...thank you."

Suddenly she heard a gurgling sound coming from him. A few moments passed and his body weight pressed into her so hard she could barely breathe. Seconds later the gold wig she wore dampened with a thick, warm wet fluid and oozed into her nose and mouth.

Trembling she kept her eyes shut, wiped her mouth with the back of her hand and hummed a nursery rhyme she'd been taught. "Baa Baa black sheep have you any whores? Yes, sir, yes sir, three rooms full. Some for my master, some for the lames, some for the old men who live down the lane."

Suddenly the man's limp, heavy body was pushed off of her and she could breathe again. Cool air rushed up her nostrils soothing her lungs.

Rolling to the side she gathered several quick breaths of air. When she turned back around the person standing before her sent chills down her spine.

It was Shayla and she had cut his throat open, blood gushing out of the wound.

Standing at the side of the bed Shayla dropped the bloody knife and in a zombie gait walked out the door.

BACK IN THE RESTAURANT

Gunner took a deep breath as he listened to Shayla at the restaurant. "I just wanted to help her but I wanted revenge too for the things he did to me," she cried. "I don't understand how men can pay for sex and be mad at us because they like it. It's so mean."

Gunner couldn't say much because he was also a culprit in the past.

"Anything else happen?" He asked.

"Can I get something else to drink?" She touched her lips. "My mouth is dry."

Gunner flagged the waitress over and ordered her another shot of tequila. She sipped it all and said, "I'm ready to tell you about another one." She paused. "He was the first one who lied to me about taking me and my sister away. When Bernice hung herself I blamed him so I had to do something about it."

FRANKIE'S MURDER

Frankie walked up the block leading to his apartment building without a care in the world. He just finished visiting Ajax's brothel and was on the way to his wife and kid when he was approached by Shayla from behind.

She was holding a knife and yet he didn't know until she poked him in the lower back, lightly at first.

"You know who I am don't you?" Shayla whispered closely into his ear.

"Uh…yeah, you're that pretty girl from the house." He tried to laugh. "Come on…why you doing this? You don't have to do this."

"Well why would you play with me like that? Couldn't you see the pain in my eyes?"

When Frankie tried to turn she reached up and she cut the side of his neck.

"Come on, what I gotta do?" He was certain that she wasn't as smart as he was and that he could talk her down if he tried hard enough. After all, the only thing she wanted was love right? She didn't want to take a life.

Without answering his question she pressed the blade into his throat, past the skin until she couldn't go any further. Warm blood oozed over her fingers as she made the firm gash.

When he was on the ground, dying in the hallway, she ran away.

BACK IN THE RESTAURANT

After telling him of the second murder she looked into his eyes, trying to see if he felt differently about her. "What do you have to say?" She sipped the new tequila brought over to the table moments earlier.

"I'm saying if they hurt you it wasn't your fault." He wiped her hair backward. "Now let's face this shit. I'm ready if you are."

EPILOGUE

1 ½ YEARS LATER

Shayla walked into Gunner's house. She was nine-months pregnant courtesy of a visit from Gunner at the mental institution some months back. After getting out early all she wanted was to settle down into a new life, the life she always imagined with her fiancé.

The life she imagined from her movies.

In the end she was tried for one murder and fount not guilty due to the circumstances of her life and temporary insanity. Not only did Louise testify how she was ripped from her as a baby, but also Lennon, now paralyzed permanently spoke to the horror she endured in the brothel before he was given five years. In the end she was medicated and her time was reduced.

Now in their home he walked Shayla over to the sofa and they both sat down. With his hand on her belly he said, "You gonna have that kid tonight. I can feel it."

She burst out laughing. "Don't say that. The doctor said two more days."

"I'm serious." He looked at her for a moment and then kissed her passionately. Squeezing her chin he said, "I can't wait."

She touched his hand and looked down at her stomach. "Me either." She looked out into the living room and back at him. "When she coming over?"

He removed his hand. "I told her to give me a few hours alone with you. Figured that would be enough time."

She nodded. "Good...not wanting much company now."

"She's your mother, Shay. And she represented for you majorly in court. When you needed her the most she was there. You gotta give her a chance."

"I know...just don't want it rushed that's all." She smiled at him. "So what now? With us?"

"A lot." He exhaled. "For starters we gotta set up shop for our baby. My daughter said she'll help," he chuckled "But we'll still need to get some things together."

"What about the other stuff?" She paused. "The dark part of our life that we pretending not to be real. The stuff that we both did together."

He frowned. "You not talking about...about the...killings."

"If the night covers us...why not do it again?" She paused. "We got away with it. Couldn't we do it some more?"

He chuckled hard. So hard he got up and looked down at her. "You playing right?"

Silence.

Silence.

Silence.

She glanced up at him and her response took forever. "Of course I am." She rubbed her belly. "Of course I am."

The Cartel Publications Order Form

www.thecartelpublications.com
Inmates **ONLY** receive novels for $10.00 per book.
(Mail Order **MUST** come from inmate directly to receive discount)

Shyt List 1	_____	$15.00
Shyt List 2	_____	$15.00
Shyt List 3	_____	$15.00
Shyt List 4	_____	$15.00
Shyt List 5	_____	$15.00
Pitbulls In A Skirt	_____	$15.00
Pitbulls In A Skirt 2	_____	$15.00
Pitbulls In A Skirt 3	_____	$15.00
Pitbulls In A Skirt 4	_____	$15.00
Pitbulls In A Skirt 5	_____	$15.00
Victoria's Secret	_____	$15.00
Poison 1	_____	$15.00
Poison 2	_____	$15.00
Hell Razor Honeys	_____	$15.00
Hell Razor Honeys 2	_____	$15.00
A Hustler's Son	_____	$15.00
A Hustler's Son 2	_____	$15.00
Black and Ugly	_____	$15.00
Black and Ugly As Ever	_____	$15.00
Year Of The Crackmom	_____	$15.00
Deadheads	_____	$15.00
The Face That Launched A	_____	$15.00
Thousand Bullets		
The Unusual Suspects	_____	$15.00
Miss Wayne & The Queens of DC	_____	$15.00
Paid In Blood (eBook Only)	_____	$15.00
Raunchy	_____	$15.00
Raunchy 2	_____	$15.00
Raunchy 3	_____	$15.00
Mad Maxxx	_____	$15.00
Quita's Dayscare Center	_____	$15.00
Quita's Dayscare Center 2	_____	$15.00
Pretty Kings	_____	$15.00
Pretty Kings 2	_____	$15.00
Pretty Kings 3	_____	$15.00
Pretty Kings 4	_____	$15.00
Silence Of The Nine	_____	$15.00
Silence Of The Nine 2	_____	$15.00
Prison Throne	_____	$15.00
Drunk & Hot Girls	_____	$15.00
Hersband Material	_____	$15.00
The End: How To Write A	_____	$15.00
Bestselling Novel In 30 Days (Non-Fiction Guide)		
Upscale Kittens	_____	$15.00
Wake & Bake Boys	_____	$15.00
Young & Dumb	_____	$15.00
Young & Dumb 2:	_____	$15.00
Tranny 911	_____	$15.00

Tranny 911: Dixie's Rise _____		$15.00
First Comes Love, Then Comes Murder _____		$15.00
Luxury Tax _____		$15.00
The Lying King _____		$15.00
Crazy Kind Of Love _____		$15.00
And They Call Me God _____		$15.00
The Ungrateful Bastards _____		$15.00
Lipstick Dom _____		$15.00
A School of Dolls _____		$15.00
Hoetic Justice _____		$15.00
KALI: Raunchy Relived _____		$15.00
Skeezers _____		$15.00
You Kissed Me, Now I Own You _____		$15.00
Nefarious _____		$15.00
Redbone 3: The Rise of The Fold _____		$15.00
Clown Niggas _____		$15.00
The One You Shouldn't Trust _____		$15.00
The WHORE The Wind		
Blew My Way _____		$15.00

(**Redbone 1 & 2** are **NOT** Cartel Publications novels and if **ordered** the cost is **FULL** price of $15.00 **each**. **No Exceptions**.)

Please add $5.00 **PER BOOK** for shipping and handling.

The Cartel Publications * P.O. BOX 486 OWINGS MILLS MD 21117

Name: _____

Address: _____

City/State: _____

Contact/Email: _____

Please allow 5-7 BUSINESS days before shipping.

The Cartel Publications is NOT responsible for Prison Orders rejected, NO RETURNS and NO REFUNDS.

NO PERSONAL CHECKS ACCEPTED

STAMPS NO LONGER ACCEPTED

By T. Styles   305

CPSIA information can be obtained
at www.ICGtesting.com
Printed in the USA
LVOW12s1929060517
533534LV00002B/18/P